A CLUE TO THE COPPER
THE COMPLETE CASES OF SILVER SKULL

A CLUE TO THE COPPER

THE COMPLETE CASES OF SILVER SKULL

RICHARD HOWELLS WATKINS

ILLUSTRATED BY
JOSEPH A. FARREN

COVER BY
C.C. BEALL

POPULAR PUBLICATIONS · 2025

TABLE OF CONTENTS

SILVER SKULL

Once He Was Captain Roderick Hayle of the Air Service—Now He Was a Madman, Agent of Destruction, Monster of the Underworld

1

THE PRISONER FROM THE TOMBS

THREE MEN SAT knee to knee in the rear seat of an inconspicuous black sedan.

The car swept briskly out of the courtyard of the Tombs prison the moment the big gate swung open. It turned north on Lafayette Street, matching with its pace the normal speed of the early traffic on that blustery and dark September morning.

Only the middle man of the trio of passengers seemed happy. He chuckled to himself, provoking instant, uneasy side glances from the other two. And then, with a movement too swift to be anticipated, he bent his head and caught up his dark blue necktie in his teeth. He chewed the fabric rapidly, almost hungrily.

For only an instant was he permitted to grip the tie in his mouth. Then both his agitated companions laid hold of the strip of blue silk. Together they ripped it from between his clenched jaws. The man on the left used his left hand; the man on the right, his right.

The quick movements disturbed a light rug that lay over the laps of the three men. It dropped to the floor. This revealed that the man in the middle was handcuffed to the other two. The prisoner laughed jeeringly into the face of the stout, dark-complexioned deputy sheriff on his

He read dead in Hayle's
eyes. He caught up a chair

right. The tall, florid man on the other side pulled up the
rug again.

"You'll be chained to a dead man before we reach dear
old Ossining, boys," the prisoner declared. His thin, slack
lips twisted into a grimace of triumph. "I told them I'd
never see the chair."

"Gorgonzola!" snapped Deputy Sheriff Moran, the tall,
red-faced man. Yet his tone was somewhat uncertain.

"What'll we do, Pat?" quavered his dark companion. "If
he's taken poison while handcuffed to us—"

Deputy Adolph Fein's voice trailed off despairingly at
the thought of what that would mean. The car hummed
on uptown, though the driver had turned a pop-eyed face
backward for an instant. He was not happy, either.

"We'll do nothing, 'Dolph," Pat Moran stated emphat-

"Now you'll get yours, kid!" Hayle spit out

ically. Under bulbous brows he glowered at his prisoner. "This fellow's been making the Tombs a hell for his keepers with his nasty tricks and fake suicide attempts ever since he got there. He's just taking us for a ride, sort of like we're takin' him. If ever a cop-killing crook was ripe for the chair, we're tied to him."

"I don't mind killing deputy sheriffs, either, boys," retorted Captain Roderick Hayle in his high, mocking voice. "Just take a taste of that tie, will you? There's enough poison deposited in it to kill every political heel in town. I'll never reach Sing Sing."

"Unless it's rat poison you could suck it all day!" Pat Moran rasped. "Now shut up or I'll forget your hands ain't free! We're not takin' you back so the whole prison can kid us. We're going on!"

Deputy Fein, who had been perspiring profusely during this interchange, spoke up again.

"Let's be nice!" he implored the prisoner. "We're just doin' our duty, Captain Hayle, like you done yours in the Air Service before you went wrong—I mean before you got into this jam. Don't throw the hooks into us, Captain! There ain't nothing on that tie, is there?"

"Did I say there was?"

'Dolph Fein, after a bewildered glance, mopped his brow and said no more. He looked at his watch and calculated how long it would be—barring poison—before he and Pat Moran got a receipt for this fellow—the most notorious criminal of the hour, although only a cop-killing stick-up man at that.

CAPTAIN HAYLE REMAINED silent, too. He kept his head pointed rigidly straight forward, although his gray eyes flicked this way and that like those of a vicious horse as the car surged on through the morning traffic.

Cop killer and stick-up man though he now was, he had been one of the most valuable men in the army air service. His face bore a queer record of his life. His skin was of fine texture but now blotched by drink and dissipation. His nose, once a thin, prominent, slightly curved beak that had won him the nickname of "air splitter" among the flying men, was a fractured, splayed mass of cartilage above lips no longer tight and decisive. His eyes, which were direct enough in darting glance, never remained focused on those of another man for more than a scant second. Ferocity and a savage slant of glee—the evil humor that battens on human suffering—lurked in those strange eyes.

A scar that began at his ravaged nose ran up across his

forehead and disappeared in his overlong, tousled brown hair. It was symbolic, that scar—symbolic of Captain Roderick Hayle's whole ruined being—this flabby, tall, red-faced, slack-lipped wreck of a once gallant figure. He had sustained that wound and broken his nose in a terrific crash while flying through a blizzard in the Rockies in search of a lost brother officer.

As the car droned up Seventh Avenue and moved more slowly through the populous mid-town section, Hayle jerked his head—his hands being unavailable—at a famous hotel. His lips curled in sardonic humor.

"They gave me a dinner there, gentlemen, on the occasion of my clipping ten hours off the time from San Diego to New York," he said lightly. "I wish to God I'd dived my ship through the banquet hall—the groundgripping, boot-licking rabbits!"

Pat Moran grunted.

"I remember readin' about the banquet, Captain," said 'Dolph Fein politely. With a furtive glance he examined the prisoner's unpleasant face. "Ah, what a great guy you were—are—I mean."

It was not long before the ex-hero had passed through the town that had honored him—passed through it for the last time, according to the verdict of an honest jury and the sentence of a pompous judge. Now he was honored in another way—by being handcuffed to no less than two deputy sheriffs, a rare distinction for a prisoner.

The car spun into Yonkers and on up the highway that paralleled the river. Without a halt it passed through town after town, and gradually something like open country occasionally supplanted the neat but uninspiring suburbs.

Captain Hayle had relapsed into utter silence.

Though his face still required occasional drying with his handkerchief, Deputy Fein now ceased to look at his watch. The chauffeur had recovered his poise. Pat Moran was as immobile as a statue of blind justice.

Once after a sudden gust of wind shook the car Hayle glanced through the rear window. Both deputies were instantly alert. But the road was empty behind them. The ex-aviator was looking up at the wind-swept sky.

"A gusty southeaster and a very low ceiling, if that means anything to you," the prisoner said. He glanced at Fein with malicious eyes. "Now, if a ship came diving out of those clouds at this car—" he murmured.

"Fat chance!" grunted Pat Moran. "Didn't even your own two buddies give you up—bein' tired o' your cranks an' general savagery? Who'd rescue you?"

"I am rescued—as far as the chair's concerned," Hayle stated in a solemn voice that made 'Dolph Fein writhe in his seat. "Did I forget to tell you that?"

"One o' these days you'll run out of Gorgonzola," Moran said and the three were again silent. Ossining was getting close. But to Deputy Sheriff Fein the car seemed merely to crawl. Again he glanced covertly at his prisoner.

His heart jounced in his chest at what he saw.

The battered red face of Roderick Hayle was slowly assuming a muddy color.

The big scar on his forehead was almost purple. His eyes were half open and the pupils were visible, languidly staring ahead. He seemed only half conscious. His mouth was slightly open, as if his lips had been pulled apart by his sagging chin.

Deputy Fein emitted something between a gulp and a groan.

"Pat!" he muttered.

Moran's head twisted instantly; his free right hand lunged instinctively toward his hip pocket at the urgency of that single syllable. Then he caught a glimpse of the prisoner's face and shoved his gun back into its holster.

Hayle was swaying a trifle now, with the swaying of the car. His face, like the scar, was turning purple. But his eyes remained drowsily open, though they seemed to focus on nothing.

"Stop!" snapped Pat Moran to the driver.

2

THE EMPTY CUFF

DEPUTY SHERIFF MORAN took a long, suspicious look around at the empty road even as the car shuddered to a halt. Roderick Hayle lurched limply forward under the impetus of momentum. The handcuffs cut at the wrists of the deputy sheriffs and they grabbed at him, pulling him back onto the seat.

"A doctor!" Fein wailed. "We got to get him to a doctor—quick! If he gets away with suicide—"

Pat Moran was already standing up, opening the door of the car.

"If it's poison he'll be dead before we dig up a doctor," he snapped. "We got to get the stuff out of him first. Ease him out!" Handicapped by the handcuffs, the two deputies struggled, panting, apprehensive, to get their sagging prisoner out onto the damp grass. The chauffeur scrambled off his seat and helped them.

"Keep your eyes peeled, 'Dolph," Pat Moran muttered, still eying the road and the country round about with fiercely challenging eyes. "This bird has no friends—unless he's bought some,"

There was a shallow ditch between the shoulder of the road and a low stone wall which defined the limits of a bedraggled and unpruned apple orchard. On the other side of the road was rising ground, sparsely covered with saplings and brush that bent and thrashed in the gusts of wind.

They lowered Hayle's unresisting body to the roadside grass, face down. Pat Moran turned the prisoner's purple face to one side, and pried open his mouth. Then he caught up a stem of goldenrod and thrust it down Hayle's throat, tickling him with more vigor than finesse.

The treatment brought instant results. Hayle retched.

Pat Moran spoke over his shoulder to the gaping chauffeur.

"Breeze to the nearest town and try to pick up a doctor, Black! Don't come back without one. Tell him to bring along a stomach pump!"

"In the car?"

"Hell, yes! Get going!"

Again he plied the stem of the weed. Save for the violent, spasmodic heaving, Hayle showed no signs of life. Pat Moran, staring at him with slitted, suspicious eyes, noted that he was not now so purple in the face.

The deputy raised his head in growing indecision, but the sedan was already in motion.

"We might ha' taken a chance on rushing him on to town in the car," Fein muttered, reading his partner's uncertainty.

Moran did not answer at once. He motioned toward Fein's pocket.

"Take this cuff off me," he commanded his brother deputy. "I'm goin' to revive this guy if I have to drown him. It'll be commendation for us if we handle this thing right—an' by ourselves."

Fein hesitated, but voiced no objection. The two officers had exchanged handcuff keys, just to make things more complicated, and now Fein found the key and released Moran from the bracelet that chained him to Hayle.

Moran stood up, glanced at the muddy water in the ditch and then further afield, as if looking for a house.

"The mud won't hurt him," Fein insisted anxiously. "He's goin' to be dead before he could get typhoid, anyhow, ain't he? Don't go trailin' away for water an' leave me alone with this guy. Here!"

He thrust the key he had just used toward Moran. "You keep it!" Fein insisted. "Now you ain't tied to him you ought to keep both them keys."

"Don't get nervous!" Moran growled. "I ain't going fifteen feet." He took the key, picked up Hayle's felt hat, peered into it, and strode toward the drainage ditch.

Fein, on his knees, stared uneasily at the man on the grass. Then he rolled Hayle over onto his back and felt his pulse. He could feel the steady throb of the pumping heart, but whether it was too fast or too slow was beyond the deputy. It seemed sort of fast—no fluttering uncertainty about it, anyhow. He edged away from the prisoner; then, with a grunt, as he felt the jerk of the handcuff, remained still.

In another thirty seconds Pat Moran was back with the hat brimming with water. He stood for a moment at Hayle's feet, intently examining the scarred, mottled face and the half open, unblinking eyes.

"Lift his head," Moran commanded. "If he's goldbricking me I'll make him wish he was all cuddled up in the hot chair."

HE DROPPED TO his knees and brought the dripping hat toward Hayle's face. Fein propped up his head.

Suddenly Hayle's right leg flashed into action. It doubled up; then shot out like a released spring. The hard leather heel smashed against the point of Moran's chin like a mallet.

The big deputy went over backward in a heap, arms limp as ribbons. The felt hat plopped onto Hayle's chest, drenching him.

Fein uttered a yell; conquered his impulse to leap to his feet and dived for his gun.

But Hayle, with a twist of his body, was on his knees. His evil, triumphant face glared into Fein's. His free left hand snapped up over his head. The empty handcuff that Moran had slipped still dangled from his wrist. Even as Fein pulled his gun, Hayle's hand and the empty metal circlet lashed down on Fein's head.

The deputy reeled, but gamely tried to aim his automatic. Again and again Hayle whipped the handcuff down on Fein's skull. Mercilessly he beat all resistance, all consciousness, out of the man. And then his hand darted out and with a jingle of the cuff closed around the barrel of the automatic in Fein's nerveless fingers.

Pat Moran was crawling stupidly to his feet. He was fighting his way back to consciousness to combat some dreadful happening—something that he could not remember.

In another moment his vision cleared enough for him to see Roderick Hayle. His terrible face twisted in a sardonic grin, Hayle knelt by the prostrate figure of Fein, to whom he was still securely handcuffed. There was an automatic in Hayle's fingers. The empty handcuff that dangled from his wrist troubled his handling of the weapon not at all.

Pat Moran was looking into the muzzle of that gun, not seven feet from him.

"I'll have those keys, Sheriff," Hayle said softly. "Don't make any mistake about which pocket they're in, either."

On the road a truck that had been travelling southward at thirty-five slowed suddenly as the driver got a glimpse of that roadside tableau. Moran fumbled awkwardly, lengthily, in his pocket.

The pistol in Hayle's fingers bellowed and leaped. The truck lunged forward again, lurching violently as the driver stared at the starred glass of the windshield.

Then, crouching, the man stepped on the throttle.

The truck dwindled in the distance. Pat Moran looked again into the glowing gray eyes of Roderick Hayle.

He pulled out the keys; then slowly took a step forward.

"Toss them—gently—toward my knees," Hayle commanded.

Moran stared at him, weighing the keys in the palm of his hand, gauging the distance between them. "Ye didn't poison yourself, then," the deputy muttered stupidly. "A trick, huh?"

"I held my breath, Sheriff," Hayle replied with a twist of his lips. "That produces all the effects of strangulation or respiratory paralysis—if you've got the will to keep on long enough. Now about those keys?"

The fingers holding the pistol tightened perceptibly.

With a curse Pat Moran flirted his hand. The keys shot into the air and dropped somewhere in the deep grass of the orchard. Simultaneously the defiant deputy leaped sideways and dived toward the ditch.

Hayle fired once.

Moran, a hurtling bunch of purposeful muscle, folded up in the midst of his plunge. He thudded to the ground. His body hung poised at the top of the bank above the rushing water. Hayle looked at him carefully.

There was no fake about that limpness. The man had a bullet through the side of his head, and since Hayle had fired while kneeling, the bullet's course was upward through Moran's brain.

Without a single glance toward the orchard where the keys had dropped, Hayle hitched around toward the unconscious Fein.

"Inconsiderate of your buddy Moran," he murmured. Rapidly he searched the unconscious Fein until he found an extra magazine of cartridges for the automatic. Then he stretched out Fein's handcuffed wrist on the grass, as far away from his own linked arm as he could get it.

With keen concentration, he levelled the heavy caliber automatic at the small bones of the deputy's wrist.

"Sorry I haven't got a knife, Sheriff," he muttered ironically, and his finger squeezed the trigger.

3

"DIRTY WEATHER—FOR DICKS"

BERT KINGSLAND, PROPRIETOR of the Kingsland
Aerial Transportation Co., laboriously two-fingered a
typewriter in that corner of the huge tin hangar which
was, by virtue of a battered desk, the general offices of the
company.

The southeast wind boomed and thundered against the
sides of the big shed. Now and then a volley of rain crack-
led over it. Kingsland, almost under the wing of one of his
two housed airplanes, ignored the gale completely, since
he had both feet on the ground. The typewriter was much
harder to handle than a ship, and Bert Kingsland concen-
trated. His was the only activity in the hangar on that dud
flying day.

Once he looked up, frowning, for it seemed that the
diffused gray daylight from the window had been interrupted by a shadow. But he saw nothing to account for the
momentary gloom, so toiled on at his letter. Engrossed, he
never heard the hangar door slide open a few inches.

When he looked up it was at the tall, drenched figure
of a man who held an automatic on a line with his head.
This man had a battered, ruined face and infernal brilliant
eyes. From each of his wrists dangled the empty circlet of

a handcuff and the one trailing from the right hand was still streaked with red.

"What the hell!" muttered Kingsland.

The intruder nodded toward the workbench.

"Get yourself a hacksaw out of that kit, unless you think you can bite these things off, kiwi," he commanded casually.

Bert Kingsland looked hard at the gun and harder at the adamant face of Roderick Hayle.

"I'm a pilot—not a kiwi, mister," he said curtly. "And I'm no mechanic, either."

"I can saw 'em off myself—if you don't want to," Hayle said softly. "Make up your mind, will you? I'm pressed."

The pilot did not flinch at the tightening trigger finger but he moved slowly to the bench. He looked longingly at a heavy S wrench, but it was the hacksaw that he picked up.

Hayle laid his left arm on the bench. He drew the pistol back until his right hand was braced steadily against his ribs.

Kingsland started work with the saw. He moved it back and forth at a sluggish rate.

Suddenly Hayle lunged forward and tapped him on the nose with the barrel of the pistol. Kingsland started back. The saw fell with a clatter as he raised his hands to his face.

"If you want your face and mine to look like maps of the same country keep on dawdling," Hayle said. "Did I say I was in a hurry? Jump!"

His face was merciless; his eyes blazed with blood lust.

Though no coward, Kingsland speeded up his sawing. The blade cut steadily through the hardened steel. At last the cuff rattled to the floor.

Hayle shifted the pistol to his unmanacled hand without a word and extended the other.

With drops forming on his face and blood dripping from his nose, Bert Kingsland worked on. The second handcuff was severed more rapidly than the first. Occasionally he ventured to dart a glance at the ravaged countenance of the man with the gun.

"Good!" said Hayle, as the cuff parted. He bent, picked up the broken pieces and stowed them in his pocket. "I'll make a mech of you yet. Now move!"

Under his gun he shepherded Kingsland to the front of the hangar. There he inspected the first ship, a conventional three-seater biplane.

"Anything wrong with this one?"

"Sure," said the pilot sullenly. "The dihedral's sour and the timer's shot. Nothing could take off in this gale."

Hayle squinted briefly along the wing. Then, still with his gun bearing on Kingsland, he climbed up for a quick inspection of the motor and the gas and oil gauges.

"Not even a good liar," he said grimly, descending. He kicked the pilot squarely off his feet. "Shove a dolly under that tail, you!"

Bert Kingsland got up, wide-eyed, staring. This man knew something about ships—perhaps he knew plenty. He obeyed. Hayle, sharp-eyed, vigilant, pulled Bert Kingsland's flying suit and helmet from their hooks. He put them on while he superintended Kingsland's efforts. Then he strapped on a parachute pack, adjusting the harness with practiced fingers.

"A HELL OF a break you're giving a brother pilot!" Kingsland grumbled. "You'll wreck—"

"You don't know all the bad news yet, dearie," said the fugitive mockingly.

Under terse direction Kingsland opened the door. Then, straining at the dolly while Hayle pushed with one hand, he wheeled the plane out onto the concrete apron in front of the hangar.

Hayle climbed into the pilot's cockpit without ever taking his eye off the owner of the ship. Under the gun Bert Kingsland swung the prop and Hayle revved up the motor. Bitterly Kingsland stood by, bending to the blast and listening to the motor hit on eight cylinders as the man in the cockpit warmed it up.

Gust after gust, shrieking around the hangar, shook the wings of the plane and set it lifting on its tires, but Hayle paid not the slightest heed to this. His attention was on Kingsland—and on the road that ran along one side of the field.

Suddenly he swung out of the cockpit, dropping down almost on top of Kingsland.

"You won't get five feet off—you won't make the edge of the field!" the owner of the ship bawled in an uncontrollable burst of anguish. "I'm almost willing to see you crack my ship—for what it gets you, damn you!"

Hayle grinned at him. "What gets me—gets you!" he snapped. With a darting movement of the arm he smashed Kingsland on the head with his automatic.

The pilot dropped to the concrete without a sound.

Roderick Hayle lifted him. With a grunt he swung the limp aviator up onto the edge of the forward compartment, under the wing. He toppled the man into the cockpit with another shove, rolled shut the wide doors of the hangar, and leaped up into the pilot's seat. He settled down on his 'chute pack; then paused to cinch on the safety belt.

In another instant he opened the throttle. Blaring defiance, the ship rolled sluggishly into the southeaster. With his strong, sensitive hand on the throttle Hayle poured gas into the motor, stirring it to shrieking power. The ship lunged ahead. The pilot peered over the edge of the fuselage, alert, confident, despite the menace of the gale.

The ship was cutting diagonally across the field. The road, with a line of trees along it, loomed ahead. But with the wind surging past the wings like a solid current of tidewater the ship was already bouncing and swaying lightly as it rushed along, neither on the earth nor in the air. With his elevator Hayle forced the wheels to remain on the beaten grass as long as he could. Then, as a shrieking gust hit, he eased back the stick.

The ship leaped skyward. The gust passed; the ship dipped a wing, knifing perilously toward the ground. Hayle slapped his ailerons over and nosed down delicately. Scant inches separated him from shattering contact with the sodden ground.

The wing came up; again Hayle raised the nose of the ship with the motor revving all out. This time he got a little more height. When the next gust hit him he went out for more altitude like a soaring gull. He zoomed to the limit and jammed his plane up out of the danger zone. High into the stiffer but steadier wind further above the earth, he blared triumphantly.

He glanced over the side. Though only a few hundred feet in the air the green fields and yellow concrete road were already vanishing in a gray curtain that was slipping under him, blotting out everything. That curtain was made up of vapor from the warm ground, ragged, harried bits of low cloud and flying rain.

"Dirty weather!" Roderick Hayle muttered and showed his teeth in a grin. "Dirty weather for them—but the best in the world for me!"

Again after a glance at his compass, he stared down at the drifting, veiled earth beneath the roaring plane. An instant later he sighted the river—dull gray water crowned with curving evanescent white caps. Banking, he swung around until the nose of the ship was pointed to southward.

"Dirty weather for dicks and deputies!" he roared.

He climbed until the river was visible only in occasional rents in the tattered ranks of rushing clouds. Almost blindly he flew southward through the fluffy blankness. And as he roared down the Hudson toward the city he had quitted so recently, he divided his alert vision, between the intermittent glimpses of the earth and the complicated but most revealing battery of instruments and gauges on the broad panel in front of him.

Before he caught sight of a ferryboat below that told him he was near the city, the aching head of Bert Kingsland raised itself in the forward cockpit. Kingsland stared with mingled rage and apprehension at the man who had abducted him.

Hayle spared him no more than a glance; his lips were moving in intricate calculations involving wind drift, gasoline consumption, distance, and time. And even while Kingsland studied the begoggled face of the fugitive Roderick Hayle nodded.

"She'll do it!" he muttered. "Just a matter of following the coast line. It's the best bet I know for a hideout, a change of clothes and some money."

But he did not alter his course then to follow the coast line. Instead, he swung his ship diagonally across Manhattan, heading southeast, full in the teeth of the wind. And he climbed up through the clouds—climbed until it was certain that the blare of his motor would be utterly unheard through the thunder and pounding of the gale that beat upon the towers of the metropolis.

Steadily the ship, as solitary as a meteorite in space, bored its way higher into the racing clouds. And only those flickering needles and columns of colored liquid on the instrument board revealed that the airplane was battering its way slowly through the storm out over the open sea.

Bert Kingsland bent low in his cockpit and shielded his bare head from the blast of the propeller with his crossed arms. There was nothing to be seen ahead or below but fluffy opacity.

His face turned backward and his eyes dwelt upon what he could see of the countenance of the man at the controls. And from the intensity of Hayle's concentration upon his instrument board Kingsland derived some small hope.

"He knows where he's heading, anyhow," he muttered. "But what's he going to do with me?"

4

THE SURGEON FROWNS

GREAT CRESTING GRAY seas, moving in mighty ranks from a wrack of spume and flying spindrift to windward, flung their tremendous weight upon the granite bulwarks of a small island.

This outpost of the land, one of the hundreds that guard the rugged coast of Maine, sturdily repulsed the heaviest attacks of the sea and the gale that drove it on.

Swell after heavy swell, in endless procession, hurled itself against the low cliff and the rubble of broken rock below it, only to be dissolved into froth and vapor and to retreat, snarling, among the hollows of the rock.

Two men, the owner of this island and his son, had fought their way against the wind to the ocean side. They had come to view the magnificent conflict between sea and land before darkness dropped down on them. Now they were crouching in a cleft of rock on top of the cliff. But their eyes were no longer on the exploding swells and the streaming granite. They had turned their backs upon the thundering breakers and were staring upward, at the ragged sky above the island.

An airplane, wavering and dipping one wing and then the other, was circling the island. It had already swung twice around the roughly oblong expanse of rock, hardy grass and scrubby trees. Rising a little higher into the air, it continued to bank around, fighting the gale to remain in position above the bit of land. The roar of the wind and the thunderous bursts of the combers drowned out the sound of the motor.

"Not a chance in the world for that fellow to land here," the younger man, Robert Arnold, shouted. "There isn't a level spot on the whole island."

His father, Dr. John Arnold, nodded agreement without taking his eyes off the plane. "If his fuel supply is low he may have to try to come down, Bob," he said. "Little Quonog may look better to him than that raging sea."

"He's climbing again—look! I can see the pilot's shoulders! He's standing up!"

The airplane had plunged into the teeth of the wind, to seaward of the island. Outlined against the-livid sky, the small figure of the pilot thrust itself up out of the rear cockpit.

Even as they looked the aviator laid hands on the edge of the cockpit and flung himself head first over the side. Squirming, he dropped toward the gray sea.

Then, as the two watchers ceased to breathe, a white parachute, like some apparition of the mist, appeared from nowhere just above him. The pilot's fall was checked with a sudden, terrific jerk. The ghostly white 'chute oscillated violently; then swept down wind toward the island. It moved like thistledown before the gale, hardly seeming to descend at all.

The airplane shot on a hundred feet, broadside to the gale. A gust caught the windward wing. The plane swung up on one wingtip. It wavered an instant. Abruptly the nose of the ship whipped over after that momentary hesitation. The plane knifed downward.

In another instant it struck the sea. Amidst the breaking tops of the waves its splash was insignificant—puny. It vanished.

A wing, torn loose from the fuselage, projected for an instant from the sea, square as a tombstone. Then it flattened out. Of the plane there remained only a few bits of wreckage floating among the swells.

John Arnold and his son hardly noted that final plunge. Their eyes were all upon the perilous passage of the man under the parachute. The frail, swinging expanse of silk was being whirled toward the island at the speed of an express train—at a greater speed than those waves that burst into foam.

"If he hits the cliff—" young Arnold exclaimed in a fury of agonized impatience.

His father, small, spare, white-bearded, waited in composed silence. This was not the first time, nor the hundredth, that Dr. Arnold had seen a life swing in the balance. Many a time the life had depended upon the skill of his own hands—the lightness of his touch upon an exposed, living brain—the sureness of his eye where a slip of one tenth of an inch meant death. He could wait the outcome of a chance he could not improve with the equanimity of experience.

The gale-driven parachute swept on.

The swaying figure, trailing at the extremity of the shrouds that held him, cleared the top of the cliff by ten feet. The parachute leaped strangely skyward in the uprush of air over the cliff. Then it dropped again and swept on inland.

The dangling pilot's hands were working at his harness. Now he lithely climbed the shrouds.

The silken, distended fabric spilled a trifle of wind as he pulled on the ropes; man and parachute lurched toward earth.

The man crashed against a stunted, bushy pine tree—one of a tiny grove half sheltered by a rocky slope beyond. The flying parachute dragged him on over the springing top of the tree. He swung downward; then brought up against another young tree with a thud.

The parachute lunged on, rising above the reaching tops of the scrubby evergreens. But the man clung to the little tree. He had released himself from the driven 'chute.

Young Arnold went dashing toward the aviator. Dr. Arnold followed hardly less rapidly, despite his white hair. There might be something a surgeon could do, now.

BUT RODERICK HAYLE was on his feet. Bent, swaying, he stood still. Then, swinging his arms, he took a few uncertain steps this way and that, as if groggily trying out his limbs.

"Hurt?" asked young Arnold.

The pilot stopped and turned toward him. There was something like displeasure in his eyes as he glanced keenly at this sudden young man.

"Hurt?" he repeated, as he jerked off his helmet. "I've stopped harder trees than that. Too bad I ran out of gas and had to wreck my ship. But I guess I'm not hurt."

Dr. Arnold had arrived by then. The short, bearded surgeon's quick brown eyes traveled rapidly over the body of the aviator, noting the manner in which he stood, the evenness of his utterance, the steadiness of his eyes.

"Anyone else in the plane?" Robert asked.

"Luckily—no," the pilot answered. "That was why I had to bail out."

"I wouldn't have said you could escape without breaking a few ribs or an arm," Dr. Arnold put in. "You have good stout bones in your body, young man."

The aviator laughed briefly. He raised a hand to his deformed nose and touched the scar that ran above it back into his hair. "Not so stout that an airplane crash won't smash them, Doctor," he said. "I can see that you've spotted some of the results of my last real crash. My skull was cracked, Doctor—but it's as good as it ever was."

John Arnold's face creased in a quizzical frown at being addressed by his title. "You know me?" he asked. "Or is it by guesswork or deduction that you place me as a doctor?"

The blemished countenance of the aviator was improved by a smile.

"I know of you, Doctor," he said. "My friends—I was a transport pilot on the Chicago run—were going to call you in to push my brains back into my head after the crack-up. But a surgeon nearer at hand did the job. Yes, Dr. John Arnold is quite well known in flying circles. And I suppose I'm on Quonog Island, your Maine retreat?"

The kindly little surgeon nodded, still faintly perplexed. "This is my son, Robert," he said, laying a hand on the shoulder of the young man. "On his way to become a surgeon, too, but not quite there yet. I think you'd better come up to the house with us."

"My name is Wall—Henry Wall, gentlemen," Roderick

Hayle stated. "Naturally I'll be grateful for your hospitality. I was flying from Bar Harbor down to Portland and used more gas than I'd figured on in bucking this gale."

He talked on, cheerfully, killing possible questions with his loquacity as they put their backs to the gale and walked up over the edge of the island. On the more sheltered side, at the edge of a tiny, almost land-locked bay that was already in twilight, they looked down upon two big cabins, built of undressed logs, and separated from each other by quite three hundred yards. Around this bay the land was low and shielded by hills, so that trees and bushes grew boldly and in an abundance not found upon the higher ground.

The pilot stopped, gazing down upon the cabins. Two furrows ranged themselves upon either side of the scar on his forehead.

"I saw a feature story in a Sunday newspaper a while ago describing you rather flamboyantly as the hermit of Quonog Island half the year, and the brain surgeon of Manhattan the other half, Doctor," he said.

Dr. Arnold frowned, though he answered politely enough. "I regret that sensational article, although I could not stop its publication. No, I am hardly a hermit, though I devote a few months a year to research and meditation on surgical problems on this island. I live here alone with a cook and a Chinese servant, except when my son finds time to visit me."

Young Arnold grinned. "And I'm afraid that you'll live here too, for a few days, Mr. Wall. The old man on the mainland who makes two trips a week out to Quonog in his gasoline launch doesn't risk his boat in any kind of rough weather."

"Hope I won't be too much of a nuisance," the pilot said politely, and the surgeon reassured him with more than conventional words.

Roderick Hayle looked again at the two log houses.

"It is hard to believe that on this sizable island there are only four persons besides myself," he said, and his words were a question.

"Ordinarily there are only three," Dr. Arnold replied patiently. "One servant would be ample to look after me but my intelligent Chinese houseboy is useful as a laboratory assistant as well. That smaller cabin is my laboratory and study."

"Ordinarily three—now four," Hayle said, nodding. "The newspaper said three, too."

For a fleeting moment Dr. Arnold's grave, kindly countenance reflected faint surprise at this sustained if covert inquisitiveness.

"You may count us, if you wish," he suggested a trifle dryly, and Hayle immediately changed the subject. But though he talked of his experience in the storm his brilliant eyes roved unceasingly about as they descended to the big, comfortable log building that was the doctor's retreat.

5

"HIS WRISTS!"

IN THE COMMODIOUS chamber to which he had been led by the silent, smiling Chinese servant Huong, Roderick Hayle was stripping off his—or rather Bert Kingsland's—drenched overall flying suit. He had already tucked the automatic that had once belonged to Deputy Sheriff Adolph Fein under the mattress of the bed.

Hayle took his time, and once paused to nod approvingly at himself in the mirror. "Brains," he murmured. "Better quarters than a death house cell—and a damned sight more restful. It took brains to pick a safe hideout like this out of a Sunday paper in the Tombs, and what that dumb lawyer of mine told me about this doctor."

There was a knock at the door.

"Come in," Hayle commanded.

Huong opened the door. With his inevitable smile he laid upon the bed a complete outfit of clothing. Though Hayle gave him only a glance it was a probing one. This fellow was plainly something more than the ordinary Chinese boy.

"If Mr. Robert's shoes do not fit you, sir, perhaps the slippers will serve," the servant said. "Dinner in twenty minutes, sir."

The fugitive nodded. As Huong's flat yellow face disappeared, Hayle frowned. The opening of the door had brought to him more distinctly a succession of sounds of which he had been aware only subconsciously.

It was the voice of a man talking endlessly—the rather mechanized voice of a most fluent talker.

"Radio, blast it!" Roderick Hayle muttered, and began to strip off his clothes. "Who'd figure that a medical hermit would have a set—and use it? Probably that son of his—I didn't count on him."

In five minutes he was dressed. He paused an instant to transfer the gun from under the mattress to his hip pocket. Then he hurried downstairs.

Dr. Arnold and Robert were standing together in the living room, in front of the huge fireplace. Oak logs were snapping and giving forth generous warmth. Father and son were facing an unobtrusive console from which flowed the voice:

"—but so far the search in that direction has been fruitless. One clue that—"

Politely, as his guest entered the room, Dr. Arnold crossed over and snapped off the switch.

"Don't turn it off on my account," Hayle said with obvious insincerity.

"I hope your adventure has given you an appetite?" the surgeon inquired.

"I have nothing left but my appetite," the pilot replied.

There was a moment's silence. Then Hayle spoke again, almost reluctantly, but driven on by a fear that cried out to know the worst:

"Any news?"

Robert shrugged casually. "A convict has escaped—that fellow Hayle who killed the policeman outside a Harlem chain store. He got away from two armed deputies to whom he was handcuffed, killing one and shooting off the hand of the other. Nice fellow. They're combing Westchester County for him. Wasn't that the case they tried to drag you in on, Dad?"

Dr. Arnold nodded gravely. "The defense wanted me to examine this Captain Hayle at his first trial. The question was raised that he might have suffered a brain injury of some sort in the airplane accident which ended his career in the army air service. But his attorney made a most unfavorable impression on me—a crooked lawyer if there ever was one—and I declined."

His son laughed. "Dad doesn't like to touch pitch even though it pays," he said.

"If I could have examined the man without committing myself—without letting myself in for acting as the mainstay of a false and misleading defense—I would have done so," replied Dr. Arnold. "But I had work to do—both research and operations which I hoped would be of greater service. So I decided against it."

Roderick Hayle bared his teeth in a smile. "After all, it is simpler to apply electrical treatment to these cases at the Sing Sing hospital, even if the patient invariably dies," he suggested.

Dr. Arnold frowned at the cynicism of this; then assented. "That seems to be the attitude of the state at present. But some day that may change. I—my decision in the Hayle case has troubled me more than once since then."

Again Hayle grinned, warming his back comfortably in

the glow of the flames, and shooting his swift appraising glance from one to the other.

"Probably it has troubled Rod Hayle, too," he said.

Dr. Arnold looked at him with sudden interest. His brown eyes surveyed with the piercing scrutiny of a diagnostician the wreck of a face. He had seen many such faces; he remembered having viewed photographs of one case in which the injuries were similar to those of this visitor from the sky. What case had that been?

"DO YOU KNOW Hayle?" he asked.

The aviator shook his head emphatically. "He was air service—I'm a commercial pilot. But don't think I'm trying to defend him— I'm all for giving him the heat."

The surgeon clutched his left hand with his right in the intensity of his thought. "The utter ferocity—the animal ruthlessness—of this last exploit of Hayle leads me to think that I may have failed grievously in my duty when I did not examine him," he said. "The man had an excellent record in the army, as I recall. And then—a crash, serious injuries, physical recovery but utter moral collapse— Not insanity, of course, but—"

"Maybe he had a better time after the crack up than he did before, when he was the darling of the tabloids," Rod Hayle cut in flippantly. "Maybe the accident just made him sensible."

Dr. Arnold's right hand closed on his short white beard. "You think so?" he asked quietly and then turned as the Chinese servant and laboratory assistant entered in the guise of butler.

Huong, bowing, announced that dinner was served. Dr. Arnold stood up. For an instant he did not move. He was lost in thought. Then, with an effort, he came back to his surroundings and to the curious eyes of the others. He led the way across the big living room to an alcove which in daylight overlooked the tiny bay. There a small table, set for three, awaited them.

"Dinner music?" inquired Robert. He paused by the radio. "It always gives me a kick to hear the orchestra playing at some supersuperb New York hotel when I'm up here on a desert island with the wind howling and the sea—"

"I have no objection, if Mr. Wall is willing to sacrifice his ears," Dr. Arnold said. His slim, competent fingers were twisting.

"By all means," Roderick Hayle agreed, twisting his lips into a semblance of a polite smile. "I must confess I've heard enough howling wind to satisfy me today."

Robert flicked on the switch, found a station and adjusted the volume of the gush of music. Then he joined them over the clam broth that Huong had just borne in.

"Oh!" Dr. Arnold looked up suddenly, with his bouillon cup poised. "Pardon me. Huong, I'm afraid I forgot to bring over that stuff Mary wanted for her toothache. I seem to forget cooks except at mealtimes. I hope she hasn't suffered?"

Huong did not reply for a long instant. Then, "No, sir."

"I'll write it out now, if you two will excuse me," the surgeon said. "Compound it yourself, Huong; it's simple enough, although usually effective."

Hastily he drew out a note book, wrote a few lines on an empty page, tore it out and handed it to the Chinese. "My apologies to Mary," Dr. Arnold said. "She must go to a dentist as soon as the gale permits."

Huong, bowing, departed. Roderick Hayle's eyes followed him as far as the pantry door. Then he glanced at the surgeon. Dr. Arnold was already engaged upon his broth.

The dinner continued. It included a fish course contributed by Robert's skill with a rod, but the surgeon confessed that the lamb came from the mainland. There was little conversation, for both the whistling of the gale and the strains of the orchestra made it necessary to speak too loudly for comfort. And Dr. Arnold was in turn absorbed in thought or keenly if surreptitiously observant of his guest. The meal dragged perceptibly. At last coffee was placed before them by Huong's deft hands. Even after it had been drunk, Dr. Arnold lingered at the table.

Suddenly a selection notable more for its sprightliness than melody ended with a flourish. The announcer's voice cut in. Instinctively the three men listened, held by the gravity of his tone.

"The New York state police have requested that the following special announcement be broadcast by every radio station east of the Mississippi:

" 'It is now believed that Captain Roderick Hayle, convicted murderer of a policeman, who escaped from custody after killing a deputy sheriff, has fled by airplane. Albert Kingsland, proprietor of a flying field within a mile of the scene of Hayle's escape, is missing, as is one of his machines. Employes of Kingsland are positive in asserting that he had no intention of flying in the gale now raging over the North Atlantic states. Marks of blood and filings believed to be from the handcuffs of the fugitive have been found in the Kingsland hangar. The plane was heard taking off within an hour of the time of Hayle's escape.

" 'It is considered impossible for Hayle to disguise himself successfully. His broken nose and a livid scar running from the nose up over his forehead—'"

Robert Arnold uttered a cry. He sprang to his feet, staring with wide eyes at the scarred face of Roderick Hayle opposite him. Then his eyes fell.

"His wrists, Dad!" he shouted. "Look at his wrists! Marks—the marks of handcuffs! It's—"

"Sit down!" Hayle commanded. There was a blue-black automatic in the hand that had whisked behind him for an instant. "Don't get excited. I said, sit down, kid!"

"Rob—down!" commanded his father. There was deep apprehension in his voice. He thrust out his hand to grip his son's arm. "Don't move!"

But Robert Arnold was too excited. He evaded his father's hand and, catching hold of the edge of the table, heaved it up to overwhelm the man sitting opposite him.

6

MASKED FACES

LITHELY RODERICK HAYLE leaped from his chair. The table, with an avalanche of silver and cut glass, crashed over.

Dr. Arnold, slipping out of his seat, sprang desperately at the pilot as he caught a glimpse of the unrestrained ferocity blazing in Hayle's face. But Hayle met his rush with a straight-arm thrust that sent the older man staggering. And then his gun came down in line with Robert Arnold's chest.

"Now you'll get yours, kid!" Hayle spat out.

Robert, in the corner of the alcove, read death in Hayle's flaming eyes. Gamely he caught up a chair, but before he could throw it Hayle had fired.

The flying lead crashed through Robert Arnold's heart. He collapsed, dead before he struck the floor.

Roderick Hayle rounded on Dr. Arnold. He clubbed him on the side of the head with the pistol. The surgeon dropped back into a chair. His stricken eyes were upon his son. He gasped for breath and touched his breast. Slowly he attempted to raise himself. His gaze never left the outstretched body; never for an instant turned toward the killer who stood over him with ready pistol.

The pantry door swung open. The yellow face of Huong showed in the gap. Hayle's automatic swivelled instantly.

"Stop!" he snapped. "Come in here!"

But though he fired, he had no target. Huong's head had appeared and vanished as swiftly as a snake strikes and recoils.

Disdaining the old surgeon, Hayle leaped toward the pantry door. He darted into the small room, gun raised.

The pantry was empty. He rushed on into the kitchen. That, too, was unoccupied although a woman shrieked discordantly behind the further door.

Covering the room in a single glance, Hayle ran toward that door. He flung himself at it. His leaping body thudded vainly against the panels. The heavy door was locked or bolted.

He turned and ran across the kitchen toward the pantry again. His legs felt heavy; he collided with a chair and fell. Cursing, he floundered to his feet. He reached the swing door leading to the dining alcove. His legs felt like wood; his arms were heavy. That door, too, refused now to answer to his thrust. Locked! And he had come through it only an instant before!

He lifted his heavy pistol to command the lock. Then, at the sound of voices beyond the door, he halted, listening, with gritting teeth and cruel, twisted face.

"Doctor!" It was Huong wailing. "I put it as you instructed in his coffee cup—I did!"

"It does not act at once, Huong." The surgeon's voice was shaken, weary, cracking with sudden age. "Too late! I hoped to stupefy him—but— My son! My son!"

Roderick Hayle staggered back from the door. This

drowsiness he felt was reaching upward, from his laggard limbs to his hot head; he could sense the approach of sleep even as it dulled his brain. Fiercely he struggled to think through that fog—to overcome that numbness. His invincible will rallied to his defense, but he realized that unconsciousness was only a matter of minutes.

He staggered back into the kitchen, still gripping the gun. Suddenly his terrible eyes leaped from the coal scuttle by the range to the window, and then to the pistol in his hand.

He stretched himself up to his full height beside a kitchen cupboard. He pushed the pistol over the top of a row of cans on the upper shelf of the closet. Then he caught up a lump of coal; dropped it, picked it up again with infinite pains in his sensationless fingers. Grimly, with the blood streaming down his face from his bitten lips, he crossed the room, still clutching that chunk of coal.

He staggered against the window. With a last effort he sent the lump of coal crashing through a pane of glass. It thudded down onto the slope outside. He heard it splash into a tiny arm of the bay.

He felt himself sliding to the floor. His eyes, unfocussed, wavered toward the cupboard where he had hidden the gun. His numb, bleeding lips curled in a hideous grin. Then blackness came down on him.

EONS OF UNREST—DREAMS and fears—a fantasmagoria of terror. And pain, always pain, breaking through swirling veils of vapor and nestling in his mind like some evil parasite. Always there was pain and always it was more a pain of the soul than a pain of any part of his body. He had no body—how could his body pain him?

He had no body, but still he was. He existed. But never was there anything around him that he could see or feel or touch. It was all vapor—nothingness—in which he floated, with his soul in agony.

And then, at last, it seemed to him that in the midst of that blankness now and then there appeared a segment of a face. It was a face from cheekbones to forehead. The rest was swathed in whiteness. Sometimes it was a strained, old, pallid face, wrinkled, tired, and taut. And then again it was a yellow face, smooth as the skin of an apple, with eyes that did not smoulder, like the other eyes, but peered at him with bright, impersonal interest.

But how could anyone peer at him when he was nothing but a disembodied soul in torment?

Nevertheless those two pairs of eyes, smouldering and impassive, continued to peer down at him. And another thing happened. Sometimes it was light and sometimes it was dark in the mist in which he floated. Wherever he was, day and night still alternated.

It was a matter of weeks before Roderick Hayle, emerging from unconsciousness to semi-consciousness, at last burst through the last shreds of mist. And then it was that he found himself in the bottommost depths of hell.

HUONG CAME INTO the small room in Dr. Arnold's laboratory in which Roderick Hayle lay in bed. Hayle managed to turn his heavily bandaged head far enough to see that the Chinese was clad as he often was in spotless white.

Huong's straight black hair was already crowned by a white cap, but he had not yet drawn up over his face and nostrils his antiseptic gauze mask. His black eyes examined the limp man in the bed with vivid, intent eyes. He did not speak.

Softly he drew into the room a wheeled stretcher and brought it to the side of the bed. The rubber tired wheels made no noise.

"Again?" muttered Roderick Hayle, through his muffling bandages. "Another?"

Huong, engaged with the greatest gentleness in shifting Hayle's long, emaciated body from the bed to the stretcher, did not answer. Carefully swathing Hayle in blankets he drew him out of the chamber and into another, larger chamber. From a skylight in the roof of this room autumn sunlight came flooding in, illuminating the white walls and the long white table that stood in the middle of it.

At the head of the operating table, with his mask dropped down upon his chest, stood the small figure of Dr. John Arnold. His brown eyes, enormous above his sunken cheeks, did not for an instant move to look at the stretcher or the form upon it. They were quite unfocussed, those eyes; they looked at nothing in that immaculate white room.

The surgeon did not move a muscle while Hayle was transferred by Huong from the stretcher to the operating table. He stood there, motionless, absorbed in meditation, quite oblivious of the man who lay stretched before him. At his elbow was a tray of instruments, carefully covered by spotless cotton.

Roderick Hayle, though he darted several swift furtive glances at that still figure, did not speak. Nor did he make any effort to move either his arms or his legs in feeble protest. He waited.

In silence Huong, now the anesthetist, adjusted the

funnel over Hayle's face. He turned the tap that sent ether gushing through it and narrowly observed the steady sinking of the patient into the depths of unconsciousness. Then, quietly, he touched his master's arm.

Dr. Arnold raised his mask and bent over the murderer of his son. Huong took his stand beside the tray of instruments, drawing on his rubber gloves.

7

THE HIDDEN GUN

THERE CAME A time when Roderick Hayle was not often wheeled into the operating room and put under ether.

Instead he lay in his narrow bed and stared at the ceiling or at the plaster that concealed the log walls of his room— or was it a cell? And the bleak winds of autumn moaned or roared around the cabin. He had many an hour in which to think, and he grew no fatter on his thoughts. He could remember everything, and most vivid of all were his last movements in Dr. Arnold's kitchen.

Huong attended him with all the care that a good mechanic would take of an intricate piece of machinery. Occasionally Dr. Arnold entered to examine him, always without comment. And Roderick Hayle, though his eyes were secretly or openly upon the surgeon, would not speak, either. His gaze avoided the world-weary, enormous eyes of Arnold.

As the murderer grew stronger and more aware of what went on around him, Dr. Anold asked him a question now and then about his physical condition. Then, one day, Roderick Hayle broke his silence.

"Where do you keep the cops who are watching me?" he asked in a thick, unaccustomed voice.

"There are no police on Quonog Island," replied the doctor tonelessly.

Roderick Hayle moved uneasily on the mattress.

"You mean they don't know I'm here—they don't know what happened?"

"My son's murder is known to the police," Dr. Arnold replied. "The authorities came and went weeks ago."

"And you hid me here—to carry out your revenge on me?" Hayle asked, almost incredulously.

"You may call it that."

"But your servants—do you think you can get away with this, Doctor?"

With a hand, rigidly bound—or bandaged—in voluminous layers, Roderick Hayle gestured feebly toward his swathed, ever-aching head. His eyes peered out of deep recesses in the windings of cotton, recesses that seemed like holes burned through the fabric with a white hot poker. His lips, too, were partly free of those infernal swaddling layers.

"Huong is not my servant—he is my assistant—and accomplice," Dr. Arnold replied in his inflectionless voice. "As for my cook, she was removed from the island in the grip of uncontrolled hysteria as soon as we could make the emergency signal to the mainland. She knew nothing— save that Robert had been killed by a man who betrayed us and fled."

Hayle twisted his gaunt body. "I still don't see why there aren't seven cops sitting on my chest," he muttered.

"You are quite alone with Huong and me, Hayle. The sheriff of the county of which this island is a part recovered my rowboat, overturned and adrift in the rough water between the island and the mainland. That was two days after my son's murder. The police of this state and of New York believe that Rod Hayle was drowned in attempting to escape from Quonog Island—after the murder."

RODERICK HAYLE WAS silent for long minutes.

Dr. Arnold had completed his examination and was at the door before Hayle spoke again:

"How you must hate me, Doctor, to sacrifice your law abiding conscience—to abandon your career—to square things with me."

The surgeon paused, a thin white hand on the doorknob. "I do hate you," he answered.

"And what's the big wind-up—for me?" Hayle demanded. "Something spectacular, no doubt—and painful?"

"You will see." The doctor went out, locking the door behind him.

Hayle lay still, staring up at the ceiling with brilliant, unwavering eyes. Huong came in silently, and the ex-captain ignored him. Never was a man more carefully nursed—or guarded—than the prisoner in the surgeon's laboratory.

That watchfulness was redoubled when Hayle was able to stand up and walk about. Huong was tirelessly vigilant. When he rested Roderick Hayle could not tell. He suspected, however, that the Chinese had hours of leisure during those periods in which he himself was robbed of his consciousness by the administration of ether or by hypodermic injections of other drugs.

His own recovery, he knew, was delayed by these periods of blankness. But neither the yellow, placid countenance of Huong nor the stern face of Dr. Arnold told him why this was so.

Nevertheless, he felt himself growing in strength.

"I'm coming back," he whispered to himself on the afternoon when he had four times walked the length of his room without halting. "I'm coming back."

And then the day arrived when, on command, he left the laboratory on foot and made his way slowly under a gray December sky to the other log cabin, three hundred yards away. He understood the reason for this shift. It was so that he might be more closely under the eyes of Huong as the Chinese resumed his normal duties in the surgeon's house—and the cook's duties about the kitchen.

The laboratory was closed for the winter. Dr. Arnold had deserted it altogether. Now he sat in his living room before a crackling fire, staring into the glowing heat or following with his sad, unfathomable eyes the feeble, restless movements of Roderick Hayle about the room. Arnold no longer spoke to his guest. The radio was dismantled.

Hayle was permitted to go anywhere. But though his eyes often scanned the door that led through the pantry he never attempted to enter the kitchen. The rolls of bandage, though lighter, were still upon his head. Other bandages, which had covered his feet, his hands and parts of his legs were gone.

Hayle walked. When he left the house Huong followed him. Only when he was alone in his room, which now had barred windows, did he attempt other forms of exercise, such as tensing his fingers or raising his arms high over his head, as if reaching for something.

DR. ARNOLD WAS dining alone, as he always dined now.

Huong attended him. The Chinese moved briskly in from the kitchen with a steaming dish and waited disconsolately at the elbow of the surgeon while Dr. Arnold made half hearted movements with his knife and fork. Minutes passed and the contents of the dish did not diminish perceptibly.

Roderick Hayle was not in the room. He had never dined with the doctor since that dinner which had been ended by the silken voice of a radio announcer and the roar of an automatic letting the life out of Robert Arnold.

This meal of Dr. Arnold's was no joyous occasion.

Suddenly Huong turned his head. His slanting eyes leaped to the pantry door. It had swung open.

Roderick Hayle stood in the door that led from the kitchen. He gripped in his right hand a cocked pistol. It was the weapon that he had concealed so carefully in his last failing moments of consciousness after the murder of young Arnold. The pistol nestled comfortably in his thin fingers. There was a smile on his taut lips.

Dr. Arnold turned his head as his servitor froze to the floor.

"It is time that you and I had a talk, Doctor," Roderick Hayle stated crisply. "Don't move, Huong."

He advanced steadily to the table and stood opposite Dr. Arnold, looking down at him. Behind the silent surgeon Huong stood, yellow hands limp at his sides.

"I didn't sling this out the kitchen window into the bay, as you may have thought," Hayle explained. "I reckoned that I might need it—but I never guessed how badly I would need it."

Dr. Arnold said nothing.

"Yes," Hayle muttered. "I need this gun."

"You have something to say to me before you use it?" the surgeon asked in his steady voice.

"I have." Hayle leaned forward, to look down at the unmoved, lined face of John Arnold. "I can't make you out, Doctor. For a long time I thought torture was your game—that you wanted to make me suffer as no man had ever suffered before. And you did make me suffer. Plenty!"

His fingers shook for just an instant.

"But the facts didn't quite fit the theory. And then, gradually, I came to understand the real subtlety of your vengeance. Somehow or other you have restored me to myself—to the personality that was mine before I became a killer. I am Captain Roderick Hayle of the army air service, not Rod Hayle of the death house!"

"That is so," said the surgeon impassively. "The operation was quite simple—and far from unique. That airplane accident in the Rocky Mountains in which your skull was fractured left you with a blood clot and a bit of bone that pressed upon your brain. The damage done was to the delicate centers controlling, not your physical movements, but your ideation—your thoughts. You might have become subject to paralysis, epilepsy or insanity had the clot formed elsewhere within the cranium. As it was, you became a moral imbecile, like those animal-like gunmen of whose crimes we read. It was impossible for you to distinguish between right and wrong. That power was atrophied—perhaps it was gone forever; perhaps capable of partial or complete restoration. I could not tell."

He glanced up at the tense lips of the bandaged mask-like head in front of him. "I could not tell," he repeated.

"What I did was to trephine the skull—to remove a disk of bone above the centers I have referred to. Turning back the dura mater—the hard membrane enveloping—but I need not describe the operation—"

"No," said Roderick Hayle. He gave vent to a harsh, unnatural laugh. "You need not describe the operation. I know its result. Again I congratulate you, upon the skill of your fingers—and upon the cunning of your brain. You have avenged your son!"

His voice cracked. "My memory is good!" he said hoarsely. "I remember everything—why I was condemned to die in the electric chair—how I escaped from two deputy sheriffs—and that pilot!"

He licked his lips. "I remember that pilot—the man whose ship I stole. I took him up with me, so he would not be able to give the alarm. Out above the Atlantic in the midst of the storm I rolled the ship over on her back. I had a safety belt on me; he had none. His hands clawed the edge of the cockpit before he dropped. And then your son! That's the foul sort of thing I remember—that's the hell you've cleverly pushed me down into! Memories of a fiend!"

His voice faded out in his dry throat.

8

SILVER SKULL

HAYLE STRUGGLED HARD for utterance while Dr. Arnold sat quite still. Huong was a yellow statue. Finally, with an effort that whitened his hand on the automatic, Roderick Hayle regained control of his throat.

"I know that the apologies of an animal like me—apologies for murder!—would be grotesque, so I make none, Doctor. Believe me, I have suffered—suffered more than you think. The sense of guilt is on me. The only further reparation I can make I make to you now!"

Swiftly Roderick Hayle twisted the muzzle of his automatic around. He pushed it into his mouth—jammed it against his palate—and pulled the trigger.

The hammer snapped forward with a click. No bullet tore its way up into Hayle's brain. A click—as the hammer struck the firing pin. That was all.

With a gasp Roderick Hayle cocked the automatic again.

Neither the surgeon nor the Chinese made a move to stop him. Dr. Arnold spoke coolly.

"There is a cartridge in the barrel, but there is no powder in the cartridge," he said. "We searched for that pistol and found it on the shelf. Huong made the cartridges harmless.

I could not be sure of the results of such a delicate operation, you see."

The pistol slipped from Hayle's fingers onto the table cloth. He swayed on his feet in mute agony. "I can die—you should not stop me!" he moaned.

"It is not going to be as easy as that, Hayle," Dr. Arnold stated with quiet gravity. "There is no reparation—no benefit to anyone save yourself in quitting the world at the point of a roaring pistol. That smacks more of Rod Hayle, the gunman, than Captain Roderick Hayle, U.S.A."

The tall young man put his hands to his head. "I can die in the chair—I am not afraid," he muttered. "Is that what you want?"

Slowly John Arnold stood up. He looked across the table at his patient.

"When my son—died—I was full of bitterness," he said in his low voice. "Full of bitterness, though I was almost certain that pressure on your brain—and that alone—had made you a killer. The man in me cried out for vengeance—to deliver you to the police—to send you to the electric chair. But then I revolted at the thought of piling wrong upon wrong in frantic effort to make a right. Was not I, too, guilty of my son's death, since I had refused to examine you in the Tombs? If my diagnosis were right, then you were two men—one guilty, one innocent.

"I operated upon you ruthlessly, dangerously, to kill the guilty man and revive the innocent. Have you read in the Old Testament of men possessed of devils? You were such a one. I cut into your brain to drive out the devil. Then I waited, without too much hope, to obtain a clear indication of the result. I think I have succeeded."

There was silence.

"I think I have succeeded," Dr. Arnold repeated.

He slipped his hand into his pocket and drew out a loaded magazine containing seven cartridges. This he pushed across the table to Hayle.

"If I am wrong I wish to be the first to die," the surgeon said gravely. "These are not dead bullets."

RODERICK HAYLE LAID the magazine beside the weapon on the table.

"I know you have succeeded, sir," he said. "Rod Hayle is dead. But I will go to the death house nevertheless. Who will believe that I do not deserve to die in the chair? Who will not call this a thin trick or a surgeon's delusion? And where could I hide—with my reputation—with my unmistakable, broken face—with my infamous fingerprints in every police headquarters in the world?"

"Take off the bandages, Huong," Dr. Arnold said.

The impassive Chinese moved at once. With his gentle hands he unwound the multitudinous folds that still masked most of the face of Roderick Hayle. Air, with a strange feeling of coolness, played upon Hayle's skin as the cotton fell away.

"Get a mirror, Huong," the surgeon commanded.

In an instant Roderick Hayle was staring at himself. He looked into a lean, dead-white, freshly shaven face that was not his own. It was surmounted by silver white hair. No longer did the broken wreckage of a big nose with exposed, hideous nostrils sprawl between his eyes. A straight, thin bridge, small but in no way unusual, had replaced it. There was no scar reaching up from that travesty of a nose across his forehead to his hair.

"I did not restore Captain Hayle to life to have him destroyed by the State," Dr. Arnold said. "There remained sufficient cartilage to rebuild your nose. Your chin was too damningly characteristic of you. I removed a bit of bone from the point, flattening it out. I have grafted skin from other parts of your body to your face. Your hair turned white under the stress of suffering, for I was merciless. Are you thinking of your fingerprints? I have destroyed all trace of those betraying loops and whorls with an electric needle and replaced them with skin from your own toes."

Hayle slumped into a chair. Swiftly Huong removed the mirror from his staring eyes.

"Rod Hayle is dead," the surgeon said. "Captain Hayle, the man of energy and will, is living, but must never reveal himself—in the flesh."

"Then who am I?" Hayle muttered. He touched his face with questing, uncertain fingers.

"That you must decide," Dr. Arnold answered solemnly. "But I hope you are a man who may yet help to unpile the wrongs we all pile up."

Hayle's searching fingers swept his silvery hair, until they came to the back of his skull.

Dr. Arnold nodded.

"That is a small silver plate—a safer thing than the diseased and ill-knit section of bone we removed in trephining. Within a short time your hair will grow over it. More than one war hero has such a souvenir."

"Gallant action!" Hayle repeated bitterly. "I acquired mine in a different way." With an effort he stood up. "But I'll try to justify my silver skull, sir. I belong down in the foul sink I fell into. Wrongs? There are plenty. And perhaps—knowing the underworld as I do, I can save a life or two that I might once have taken."

He picked up the automatic, withdrew the useless bullet from the chamber and clicked the loaded magazine into the handle of the pistol. There was decision in his crisp movements.

"You have my word, Doctor. While this silver skull lasts I will not be without a task."

Dr. Arnold, though his face was deadly white, thrust out his hand. Firmly he took in his own the hand of the man who was to become known in the course of his strange, dangerous and useful career as Silver Skull.

THE SECRET OF SILVER SKULL

*Rod Hayle, Hunter in the Underworld, Burns
a Fiery Trail from a Shack on the Road to
Boston to the Death House at Sing Sing*

1

THE HIDDEN AUTOMATIC

RODERICK HAYLE STROLLED at midnight along a street near the northern boundary of the city, with a peculiar screwdriver tucked in the inner pocket of his coat. His brown felt hat, tilted backward, concealed well the silver plate that replaced a circular section of his skull.

He strolled because the cop a short distance in front of him strolled. The patrolman passed, without so much as a disdainful glance, an untenanted, dilapidated service station a hundred feet from the Boston Post Road. In all that drab wilderness of signboards, old car dumps, vacant lots, tenement houses, and gas stations, this unpainted shack was the building least likely to tempt a burglar.

The cop paused a moment on the corner of the Post Road to execute an intricate juggling feat with his nightstick. Then he moved slowly southward, quite unconscious that a man for whom the electric chair had been made ready in Sing Sing death house was observing his departure with approval.

Rod Hayle stood in the lee of a dismantled gas pump until the bluecoat's sizable feet had carried him out of sight behind a monstrous cigarette advertisement. Then he slipped around to the rear door of the dilapidated filling

As Rod Hayle leaped, Vicar jerked up the machine gun

station. He took out his screwdriver, which had a handle at right angles to the point, and trained a flashlight, held in the crook of his elbow, on the door. Without haste and without lost motion he unscrewed the three screws of a padlocked staple that secured the door.

When he had taken off the staple he opened the door, stepped inside, unlocked a tightly fastened window, and came out again. He replaced the staple on the door with meticulous care and then entered the shack once more by the window. Once inside he locked the window again.

The windows were unshaded and the brilliant standard lamp on the corner of the Post Road threw a pallid radiance through the dirty panes. Without use of his flashlight Roderick Hayle moved to a tire rack that occupied one wall of the place. Gently he took down half a dozen worn and dusty tires, and then, by feeling alone, located and lifted out a section of the slanting board behind them.

Screening his flashlight, he focused it carefully before pressing the button. The white light streamed into an aperture between the tire rack and the clapboard wall of the shack.

Intently the man with the silver skull stared at the contents of that square hole. A sub-machine gun, barrel canted toward him, menaced his head, but he glanced beyond it. There was in the hiding place a small suitcase, a greasy suit of dungarees, a respectable suit of blue serge carefully folded, a set of car license plates, a safety razor, and a cigar box containing a few fine stones obviously torn from settings, and heavy chunks of queerly shaped gold and platinum. These latter were undoubtedly settings to which enough heat had been applied to render them unidentifiable.

But Hayle's slate gray eyes passed over all this stuff to bear upon another object half hidden under machine gun clips in the bottom of the hole. It was a .45 caliber automatic made of blue steel. With his handkerchief over his fingers he picked up this weapon, examined it swiftly, and then read the number upon it.

Slowly his lean lips twisted in a smile. "The gun that killed John Bland," he murmured. "I knew Art Vicar wouldn't throw away a good gat. One mistake—and a mistake that will help."

With great care he replaced the automatic. His eyes passed over the precious and easily portable loot with indifference.

Taking nothing, he put the board back and lifted the old tires up onto the rack again without disturbing the dust on top of them.

In another moment he climbed out the window. With quick fingers he hitched a doubled bit of string around the handle of the window catch and closed the window. With the ends of the string passing through the narrow space between the two weathered sashes he was able to pull the catch shut and then slip out the string. The shack was precisely as he had found it.

He had taken two steps toward the front of the old building when suddenly he stopped.

TO HIS EARS came the shrill, menacing shriek of a siren—the kind of siren used on police radio patrol cars. He located by hearing the position and course of the car. It was running northward on the Post Road—and it was running fast.

Rapidly Roderick Hayle circled the shack. In the empty lot next to it was a melancholy array of rusting, dismantled cars—a graveyard for the models of yesteryear. With that siren rising in intensity in his ears he stopped beside a dump truck with twisted frame that stood on three wheels at the very edge of the lot.

He listened, picking out of the subdued murmur of distant traffic on the Post Road the snarl of a fast-driven machine coming close. Lithely he swung himself up into the truck.

Hardly had he dropped into the discarded vehicle when a taxicab flashed into sight, cutting the corner with screaming brakes and screeching tires. From it, at the moment when it had made the curve and lost much of its speed, jumped two men. They had automatics in their hands.

The taxicab, picking up momentum under the renewed

urge of the driver's throttle foot, shot past the filling station and the dump truck. It droned away westward.

The two men, who had dropped off close to the deserted filling station, immediately dived toward shelter behind it.

The intent gray eyes of Roderick Hayle appraised them in the light of the Post Road lamps. The shrill hunting cry of the racing police car was vibrant in his ears.

"Art Vicar on deck—and teamed up with a cokey like Sleighbells Gwynne!" the man with the silver skull muttered in some surprise.

In the old days Art Vicar, the smooth and clever, had held himself aloof from drug addicts and crooks too well known to the police.

The police roadster came jamming around the corner, bouncing and rocking on the rough paving. Well ahead down the street showed the red tail light of the taxi, now shooting into another turn. The radio car accelerated.

But the vision of one of the cops in that car was quick and sure. His voice rose; his arm pointed.

The two fugitives had cut it too fine. He had seen them.

The cop at the wheel stood on his brake pedal and turned the wheel to dry-skid the car to a stop. Rocking under the strain, the car whirled, speed slackening.

Suddenly one of the overtaxed tires let go with a blast like a shotgun. The machine leaped crazily. It was beyond control.

Twice the fast whirling roadster rolled over. The two blue-clad occupants, clutching and sprawling, were flung clear of its crushing bulk as it turned turtle. They jarred on the pavement.

Only one of the two moved.

Roderick Hayle, staring down from his place in the derelict dump cart, was within fifteen feet of the nearest policeman. This man's body was limp.

The patrolman who had survived that crack-up with senses unimpaired was a good cop. He was up on his feet like a cat. Revolver roaring, he charged past the dump cart toward the two men crouching beside the filling station. Before he had taken three strides, Art Vicar, safe under cover, had dropped him with a single, hurried shot. It was all over in an instant. Vicar deserted the shack to slip behind a billboard further from the wrecked police car.

With a yell of fury Vicar's companion, the dope nick-named Sleighbells Gwynne, came rushing toward the two prostrate bluecoats. His voice, the wild motions of his thin, jerky body proclaimed the recentness of the shot in the arm that had inflamed in him the lust to kill his enemies.

"I'll finish this flatty!" he shrilled.

Rod Hayle swung himself over the edge of the dump truck. There was an automatic strapped under his left armpit, but he did not reach for it. Instead, as he hit the street, he grabbed for the hot revolver of the shot police-man. There was grim purpose in his lined face.

Bells Gwynne, face hideous with evil glee, was almost on the cop. He yelled at the sudden appearance of Roderick Hayle beside his intended victim. But, his crazy purpose unchanged by the sight of an unarmed man, he jerked down the automatic he was brandishing to bear upon the cop's heart.

The lean fingers of Roderick Hayle were already slipping around the butt of the limp policeman's revolver. Swiftly Hayle turned up the muzzle of the gun.

The revolver blared under the steady pressure of his forefinger.

Without time to fire a shot, Gwynne's rush faltered. His hands clawed and waved like the hands of a slack rope walker balancing himself. His legs buckled under him. He thudded face first onto the ground, five feet from the cop he had run to kill.

Rod Hayle flattened out promptly behind the meagre shelter of the coke addict's body. He flipped the revolver around to command Art Vicar, crouching at the edge of the billboard. At that very moment Art Vicar cut loose his automatic; not in a burst, but with a careful pause between each shot. One chunk of his lead kicked up the policeman's right foot; another nearly creased the silver plate on Rod Hayle's head.

Hayle did not fire in return.

"Stan' up an' fight!" snarled Vicar, his head darting around the end of the billboard. "Come on—whoever you are!"

"I'll see you later, Art!" Rod Hayle called softly.

Vicar for an instant offered a fair target, but Rod did not lift the cop's revolver.

"Later—Art," he repeated. "I'm saving you."

"Who the—! Is that—?"

Art Vicar stuttered incoherently at the sound of Hayle's voice. Then, without another sound from throat or gun, he departed in a sudden spurt. He ran along the inside edge of the billboard. Rod Hayle, climbing to his knees, did not speed his going with the gun. But he carefully marked the killer's course. Then he turned quickly to the sprawling figures near him.

2

THE POLICE REVOLVER

THE COP BESIDE Roderick Hayle was stone dead—one through the heart, probably. Sleighbells Gwynne, with lead in his brains, was also gone on his last ride.

With tense speed Rod Hayle wiped the butt of the policeman's service revolver—the weapon with which he had killed the cocaine addict—on the man's blue tunic. Then he pressed it into the relaxed fingers of the dead cop's gun hand.

The other patrolman, who had been knocked cold by the smash, was moving arms and legs confusedly, like a man in a bad dream. And slowly but with increasing speed the neighborhood was awakening to life.

Lights blazed here and there in the nearest tenement windows. Two cars had already halted on the Post Road at the end of the street while their hesitant drivers peered intently at the vaguely visible wreckage of the patrol car.

Flattening out again, Roderick Hayle crept into cover under the dump truck. Before the boldest driver had brought his car within fifty feet of the scene he was melting from shadow to shadow among the obscure bulks that lay in the automobile graveyard.

Shaping his course diagonally across the lot toward the

Post Road, Hayle kept on the move. His pace through the maze of rusting steel and crumbling sheet metal brought him many a bone racking hurt, but he persisted in his speed. It was in the direction of the Post Road, skirting the signboards, that Art Vicar had run.

Suddenly, from the road amidst the intermittent noise of traffic, came a sudden, emphatic command, delivered in a breathless voice.

"Stop, you! I want—"

Rod Hayle took three noiseless strides and halted beside the line of billboards. He peered through the green lattice under one of them. He was just in time to make out the darting figure of Art Vicar slipping between two signboards back into the littered lot. Vicar had found the Post Road too hot.

The man who had uttered the command was the patrolman whom Roderick Hayle had watched only a few minutes earlier that evening. He was pounding along on the sidewalk within thirty feet. Evidently the cop had run many blocks in the wake of the radio patrol car; his shoulders were heaving.

The officer jerked out his gun, fired in the air, and then put a couple more through the slot into which Art Vicar had dived. Then, panting, he charged after him.

Roderick Hayle crouched, frozen, beside the lattice, listening to the sounds of pursuit through that black labyrinth of rusty metal. Within two minutes a rush of curious citizens—motorists and pedestrians alike—poured into the lot to complicate the exhausted policeman's search.

As soon as a score of unhelpful helpers were blundering

about in the lot Roderick Hayle stepped out onto the Post Road, rubbing one shin.

"Full of junked cars," he grumbled, to a wide-eyed couple in a car that had just drawn up. "They'll never get him."

Ignoring their barrage of questions, he moved southward. At the next crossing his vigilant eyes caught sight of a man sauntering with exaggerated ease across the Post Road from the corner of the lot. Hayle saw that, despite the swagger, the man was limping slightly. As soon as the stroller had put a stream of traffic between him and the searching policeman, he dragged himself swiftly into a dog wagon.

Roderick Hayle crossed, too. He entered the dog wagon briskly and noisily. A gaunt man in a dirty apron stood behind the counter—and Art Vicar was alone in front of it.

Vicar, already on a stool, whirled around swiftly at Roderick Hayle's entrance. His dark, blunt face was as hard as quartzite. He scowled at Hayle, but without recognition of those placid, much changed features. Then he turned back to the solitary counterman, whose cadaverous face plainly mirrored both suspicion and apprehension.

Art Vicar read him in one glance.

"Been stickin' that pan o' yours out the door, hey?" Vicar snapped at the boss of the lunch car. His hand, with an ugly, short-barrelled revolver in it, drew out of his right hand coat pocket for just an instant. "Well, you, Mr. Dog Wagon—and you, customer"—his black eyes blazed for an instant at Roderick Hayle—"you both get ready to swear that all three of us been in here together for twenty minutes. That's in case a cop comes nosing in. D'you get me—or would you rather get perforated?"

"Mister, I get you!" said the lean counterman fervently. His mournful face was earnest; he drew a cup of coffee with shaking fingers and shoved it quickly toward Art Vicar. "Be drinkin' somethin', mister, it'll look more convincin'. I'm your friend, hell, yes!"

"It seems more like twenty-five minutes we three've been here," Roderick Hayle declared a trifle hoarsely. "H-how about some coffee for me, too?"

"Sort of cool, ain't you?" Art Vicar rasped.

"Cool? I'm cold—particularly my feet," Roderick Hayle declared, with a quaver in his voice.

VICAR'S LIPS CURLED in a placated though cruel grin.

"Come closer, both o' you," the stick-up man commanded. "I'd hate to only half kill either o' you guys."

With his left hand—his right had sunk with the revolver into his coat pocket—he picked up his coffee cup.

Roderick Hayle moved nearer him and stretched out his hand for the second cup that the sad and worried counterman had filled. He lifted it halfway to his lips; then, with a flick of his wrist he sent the heavy stoneware cup crashing against Art Vicar's temple.

The man went backward off his stool. He hit the floor with a thud. Hot coffee deluged his face, but he lay quiet and unblinking. There had been power behind that thick cup.

With a grunt of relief the counterman started toward the door. Roderick Hayle's left hand straight-armed him against his coffee machine. In Hayle's right was his automatic.

"Back up!" Hayle commanded. "That sap on the floor is

only studying to be a gunman. I'm the real article with the diploma. Looking for proof?"

The gaunt counterman waved his hands high. "I believe you!" he mumbled. "Cripes, what a night this is!"

Roderick Hayle bent over Art Vicar and lifted him up. With a swift marshalling of his strength he swung the limp killer over the high counter and let him drop with a thump to the floor behind it.

"Business as usual for you!" he commanded the counterman. "My friend and I are going to be engaged and exclusive behind this nice high counter—in the corner here. You're all alone and you don't know anything if anybody comes in. Right?"

"Don't kill him in here, mister!" the counterman implored. "You look like a real nice fella to me; if you're bumping him walk him out o' here first. You got no idea what the cops do to a guy that gets a murder done in his wagon. Be nice, brother!"

"He's safer than if he were in bed," Roderick Hayle assured him curtly. He sat on Art Vicar's chest and rapidly went through his pockets. There was surprisingly little save the sizable automatic and the stubby revolver. In fact, beyond cigarettes, matches, keys, thirty-eight cents in coins and twenty-seven dollars in bills there was nothing but a telegram. That was addressed to A.V. Victor, one of Art Vicar's aliases, at the Hotel Beaulieu, Seventh Avenue near 52nd street. It had been filed the day before at Aiken, South Carolina, and read as follows:

Isaac receiving gifts to-morrow. Am returning Tenth Avenue.

"Jud."

Roderick Hayle looked more intently at that modest signature, "Jud," than at the message.

"So Art is still using that sneaking rat Jud Beltz—when he isn't working with Bells Gwynne," he muttered, as he put the telegram back into the unconscious crook's pocket. "No wonder he's down to $27.38."

Rapidly he took an impression of four keys in Vicar's bunch with a chunk of wax already warm in his pocket.

He straightened up under the wondering eyes of the counterman. "I'm accepting this little contribution," he said, thrusting the cash into his pocket. "If you don't want holes in your dog wagon and epidermis you'd better take the cartridges out of those guns of his before he comes out of it."

"You goin' to leave me here with him?" the counterman muttered in a panic. "Say—listen—"

"You've got plenty of armor plate coffee cups, haven't you?" Roderick Hayle inquired. "He's reviving already. I wouldn't risk calling a cop now if I were you. I'd hate to see my buddy arrested. Understand? I might come back if you had him pinched. Tell him I paid for his coffee."

He put a dime on the counter and stepped casually out into the night. The counterman stood transfixed, staring. The brown felt hat of the man who had just departed had worked forward on his head a bit—just enough to reveal a tiny crescent of silver, like a new moon, on the back of his skull.

Short though Hayle's stay had been, the Post Road now was almost black with halted cars. The manhunt was on, but it would be as easy to find a particular blade of grass on a lawn as a wanted man in that mob. Roderick Hayle walked briskly northward on the avenue and turned into the street of the dilapidated service station.

The wrecked radio car still lay where it had stopped rolling. Three reserves from the local police station were keeping the crowd away from it and the two blanket-covered bodies.

Roderick Hayle's gaze was directed toward the dark, paintless gas shack. Although two detectives were already at work sizing up what had happened, they paid no attention to the building. Plainly it had no significance in their eyes.

One man among the milling spectators did, however, display some slight interest in the gas station. Roderick Hayle, circulating in the crowd, caught sight of this fellow as he stood, back to the shack, surreptitiously twisting his head to peer in through one of the dirty windows.

That movement was not the bold, curious stare of a gawker or amateur sleuth; there was something furtive and stealthy and purposeful about it.

Hayle moved nearer, keeping his head bent on his chest so that his tall form would not loom above the others around him. At twenty feet he recognized the squat, bow-backed figure.

"Lump Engel," he muttered to himself. Of old he had known that heeler and spy for an invisible and formidable master to linger on the scene of more than one lucrative crime. "Lump—just taking a little look-see as usual for the Copper. It must be for the Copper. Lump would never show himself near where a cop had been killed unless he was acting under orders.

"The Copper wants to know what happened to Art Vicar to-night. Well, Lump won't find out."

Quietly he drifted out of the crowd and back to the Post Road.

"The Copper can wait," he told himself. "I've a more pressing job on hand."

Rapidly he headed northward, away from the shack and the dog wagon.

3

"THE SENTENCE STANDS"

A SANDY-HAIRED YOUNG man sat in a rather narrow cell with his long body hunched up over a small drawing board.

On that board was a sketch of a cantilever bridge which, despite its roughness, revealed plainly the professional touch of an engineer. And there were certain original details about the bridge that likewise indicated the young man's vocation.

Although Vincent Harvey's attention was focused upon his drawing, nevertheless there was something strained and forced about that fixity of interest. And when a footfall sounded in the corridor outside the cell he was on his feet in an instant, facing the corridor tensely.

The warden of Sing Sing, gray-haired, quiet of manner, stood outside his cell.

All color was drained from Harvey's face; he supported himself by clutching at the bars of the door. The drawing board lay on the floor.

"All right," he said hoarsely. "You can tell me."

Slowly the warden shook his head. "I'm sorry, Harvey," he said. "The court has refused to grant you a new trial. There is not enough new evidence to justify reopening the case."

"Then—"

"The sentence stands."

"And that means—when?"

"Thursday night."

Vincent Harvey sat down again and automatically picked up his pencil. He wiped his wet forehead with a sweep of his sleeve and lifted the drawing board to his lap.

"Thanks, warden," he said a trifle shakily. "You'd think that after ten months of this I'd get used to the idea of dying in the electric chair for a murder I didn't commit. But somehow I can't."

Again with obvious effort, he fixed his eyes upon the sketch and waited for his hand to steady. Outside the cell door the man whose duty it was to superintend his execution stood still, without speaking.

Vincent Harvey gripped his pencil more tightly in his quivering hand.

"No nerve left—but plenty of nerves," he said, with a wry smile.

The warden did not answer. He was gone.

THERE IS A beer joint—the owner is hesitant about calling it a saloon and certainly it is no garden—opposite a red brick tenement on Tenth Avenue. It is in the heart of a neighborhood that teems with action on a Saturday night. The people residing thereabouts are not noted for either wealth or gentility, but no one can gainsay that there is life in them.

Amidst all this come-and-go and buzz and shout on the avenue Roderick Hayle sat at a table close to the window. Nobody was surprised that he kept his hat on securely, for nobody in the place went hatless.

Although the evening newspaper he read was full of most interesting news to him, Roderick Hayle gave it only one eye. He devoted the other to the doorway of the red brick tenement on the opposite side of the avenue. People came and went constantly through that doorway, but not one of them got more than a single, narrow-lidded glance from Rod Hayle. One look—then back to the newspaper. He smiled a trifle grimly at the principal headline:

RADIO POLICEMAN KILLED
AFTER SHOOTING ROBBER

Just before their dramatic arrival in the taxicab, Art Vicar and Bells Gwynne, it appeared, had stuck up a limousine bearing toward Greenwich, Connecticut, a party of bejeweled ladies and bemoneyed men who had attended a performance of Thais at the Metropolitan. A radio car on patrol in Bronx Park came slowly down the road in which the robbers' taxicab had forced the limousine to a halt. The crooks abandoned the knock-off with great alacrity, but in the chase the taxi had failed to shake off the police car.

Rod Hayle, glancing over at the tenement doorway that interested him, skipped the conjectures as to what had happened in front of the filling station where the radio car had been wrecked. Naturally the detectives had decided instantly that the dead policeman, Patrolman John McQuade, had killed Belle Gwynne, since the cop's revolver was still clutched in his hand and a bullet from it was lodged in Bells' head.

Tests by the Bureau of Ballistics showed that it had not been the dope addict's gun which had fired the bullet that killed McQuade. Therefore the other robber was being sought as the slayer. Patrolman Henry Scott, driver of the radio patrol car, who had been knocked unconscious in the accident, had been able to tell nothing of importance. The number of the taxi was unknown.

"Was this hold-up of the opera party," the newspaper inquired in startled italics, "one of those sudden, lucrative, and frequently murderous crimes which the elusive, shadowy Copper is reputed to inspire?"

Concerning the identity of the escaped murderer of the policeman the newspaper said nothing definite save to recall that Bells Gwynne's last appearance in the public prints had taken place a few months before when he and Art Vicar, a luridly notorious character, had been tried in General Sessions on a charge of robbery. They had beaten the case.

With this statement as a link the newspaper then turned to Art Vicar, sketching guardedly a career of trials without convictions, accusations without proof. Rod Hayle read this with more attention. Vicar, the paper said, had made one other appearance in court within the past year. That was when, as a witness, he had testified against Vincent Harvey, a young engineer who was charged with the murder of his employer, John T. Bland, head of a construction company.

"Vicar swore that young Harvey, fearing that Bland would stumble upon his defalcations, had approached him, Vicar, with an offer of ten thousand dollars cold cash to kill Bland," the paper stated. "In the witness chair Vicar described with great emotion how he had refused any part in such a crime. Although he squirmed under a hot cross-examination, his testimony convicted Harvey, who is now in Sing Sing death house awaiting execution on Thursday night."

Roderick Hayle's face was white and stern as he read the concluding paragraphs of the story.

"The defense endeavored without great success to prove that Bland's safe was robbed of forty thousand dollars on the very night on which he was slain. The attorneys contended that Art Vicar, working with the infamous Rod Hayle, now dead, had actually committed both the murder and the robbery himself and then had pinned the crimes on young Harvey when things got too hot.

"It was the type of violent crime in which 'the Rod,' as Hayle was called in the underworld, frequently participated.

"When Rod Hayle, Vicar's alleged accomplice, was drowned in a dramatic escape, in the course of which he killed three men, the city was freed of its most ruthless and successful active criminal. That legendary brain of the crime zone known only as the 'Copper' was, as rumor declares, robbed by Hayle's death of his most brilliant and reckless executive. If so, the Copper, who was never anything more tangible than a voice over the telephone, mourns alone for the Rod.

"Squealers and gossips of the dives and prisons aver that it was the Copper's elusive voice which directed Hayle's strange, sudden lust for killing into highly lucrative lines and that the Copper shared the plunder. Certainly the Copper has been more or less in eclipse since Hayle came to his end. Possibly the Copper's voice is sore; possibly he never existed.

"Captain Roderick Hayle, U.S. Army Air Service, with

a brilliant and spotless record, suddenly became the most feared and terrible figure in crime after an airplane crash in which—"

Silently Rod Hayle dropped the paper. He sat motion-less, shoulders bent a trifle, eyes fixed but unseeing upon that doorway across the street. And then, abruptly, the eyes that saw nothing focused. He stood up, his melancholy vanishing.

"We're off!" he murmured.

4

BLOSSOM'S CLUTCH

JUD PELTZ HAD emerged from the tenement. A dark, narrow-chested little man of no more than five feet, dressed in a light suit of arresting if not tasteful pattern, he stood on his doorstep, small head darting this way and that, like a robin looking for a worm.

What Jud Peltz was actually looking for were dicks. There had been several occasions in his career when he had found dicks outside his residence. They had been gazing into shop windows or loitering in doorways. On those occasions he had returned promptly and inexorably to his quarters on the fourth floor without even attempting to back-door them. When dicks were interested in Jud, he was interested exclusively in jig saw puzzles.

But Rod Hayle, issuing from the joint that was not a saloon, escaped Jud Peltz's interest though not his attention. He was much too much like a guy coming boldly out after hoisting a couple to be a dick. His prematurely white hair was invisible at that distance and the silver plate in his skull was completely hidden by his hat.

Jud Peltz moved. And when he moved it was swiftly and with precision. His loud suit somehow faded quietly and inconspicuously into the variegated raiment of the Saturday night throng with no more splash than an umbrella in London. The gaudy little man fitted his environment.

Roderick Hayle, following, paused beside a mail box. He took a business size envelope, sealed, stamped and addressed, out of his pocket and with a grave face slipped it into the letter box. Then he closed in on the little man. But, after a sudden clear view of his quarry through the shifting throng, Hayle stepped swiftly into a doorway near the next corner.

Jud Peltz's thumbs had been running nervously along his fingertips, touching one after the other. Now, with a backward glance, he shot across the street and rapidly walked eastward.

Roderick Hayle did not pursue. He knew what that nervous gesture meant. He waited in his doorway, apparently scrutinizing dimly seen name plates under the doorbells of the tenants of the house.

"Jud's on a sizable job," he assured himself. "And he's pulling his old run-around."

In seven minutes Jud Peltz was back, coming up the avenue. He had walked rapidly around the block, giving himself a chance of spotting a trailer on four sides of a square. The fact that he did not turn back to his own door told Roderick Hayle that now he was sure he was not followed.

Without hesitation, as Jud Peltz turned east again, he took up his shadowing. But he gave the flamboyantly arrayed little man a long start.

At a rapid gait Jud Peltz headed for Ninth Avenue and then turned southward. Three blocks further down the narrow-chested little crook halted abruptly in front of a hardware store show window, next to the prominent orange and black front of a busy chain grocery. His thumbs were working rapidly against his fingers.

Roderick Hayle took cover beside a news-stand under the stairs leading up to an El station. He bought a paper. He no longer watched Jud Peltz; his eyes roved along the opposite side of the avenue. For several moments he surveyed thoughtfully the three dingy gold balls outside a cheap pawnshop almost directly opposite Jud's post of observation.

The hockshop was a typical Ninth Avenue refuge of the impecunious of the neighborhood. But the owner of it, as Rod Hayle knew well, was Ike Blossom. Ike was prepared to fence anything from the Hope diamond to an Atlantic liner—if there were enough in it for Ike.

Within ninety seconds of Jud Peltz's arrival Art Vicar showed up. He came briskly northward on the avenue with a briefcase in his hand.

Jud Peltz took off his hat, looked into it and put it on again. Art Vicar, with no more than a glance across the avenue at Jud, turned into Ike Blossom's place.

Five minutes went by. Roderick Hayle shifted his position of observation to the corner cigar store on the same side of the avenue with the pawnshop.

Of a sudden Art Vicar stepped out of the pawnshop. He walked rapidly northward. He had a zipper bag, not a brief case, in his hands.

Jud Peltz dropped his hat. Instantly a taxicab parked near the cross walk of the side street suddenly shot into the avenue, against the lights.

A COP, A powerfully built six-footer, rounded the corner

out of the side street where the cab had been parked. With a glance at the red light he ran toward the running board of the taxi as it slowed in the middle of the avenue. All this happened before Art Vicar's swinging pace had taken him twenty feet from the pawnshop door.

Suddenly the door of the pawnshop opened again with a crash. A short fat man with an enormous stomach burst out onto the sidewalk. Blood streamed down his face. There was a wound on his forehead that should have killed him. From him there came a deep-throated roar of wrath. His ponderous hands were raised over his head.

Bellowing vengefully, he rushed after Art Vicar. Despite his enormous bulk he ran like a deer. His short fat legs seemed hardly to touch the pavement; an unlucky pedestrian who dodged the wrong way went spinning aside as if a car had hit him.

Ike Blossom was mad. For years he had been a god to crooks—taking what they had and tossing them back a fraction of the value of the thing they had stolen. He had bullied them and commanded them and made a fortune from them, and he had esteemed his shop and his vault the safest in New York from burglar or stick-up. Full-voiced, raging, with no more fear of Art Vicar than if he had been a pickpocket, he dashed after him. The blood dripped from his chin onto his shirt.

Art Vicar wavered on the curb an instant as he glimpsed the policeman on the running board of the taxi. The cab and driver screened most of the tall cop's body from Vicar. The bluecoat was already turning from the driver toward the shouting Ike Blossom.

Suddenly Art Vicar jerked his head upward. An elevated

train was roaring into the station over him. He whirled around, dashing back toward the elevated stairs. His lithe body was moving fast as he swerved to dodge the broad chest and clutching hands of Ike Blossom.

Roderick Hayle did not move a muscle. He waited, alertly.

Ike Blossom's fat, vengeful hands lashed out at Vicar as he started to leap up the elevated stairs.

Snarling, dodging, Vicar jabbed an automatic at Ike Blossom's huge stomach.

The fence's thick fingers grabbed at it. His right hand closed on the weapon's barrel with a rigid, unbreakable grip. His left clutched at the leather zipper bag.

Art Vicar, one eye darting toward the policeman running from beside the taxicab, pumped the trigger of his automatic frantically. Hot lead poured into the pawnbroker's vitals before he could twist the gun.

Ike Blossom's roar became a bubbling wail. He swayed on his feet and that terrible clutch on the pistol became even tighter. It was the grip of death. He tottered backward.

The automatic and the bag were torn from Vicar's fingers by the weight of the pawnbroker's great, falling body. He twisted around and sprang up the elevated stairs empty handed. But before he had mounted eight steps his empty right hand was thrusting toward his coat pocket. With bared teeth he glared down at the tall patrolman.

The big cop, running, was pulling his revolver out of the holster in his right hip pocket with fumbling, clumsy fingers. He charged on at a lumbering gait. Whether or not the slow, heavy bluecoat knew he was easy meat for the quick-shooting robber he advanced gamely, at his best pace.

Rod Hayle took three flashing steps toward the prostrate body of the dying pawnbroker. Ike Blossom had dropped the automatic and bag now, to paw unavailingly at the stair railing. He looked grotesquely like an enormous tortoise, helpless on his back.

At the top of the stairs, near the turn to the ticket office, Art Vicar paused. His body was shielded behind the corner; only his head and the queer, short-barrelled revolver in his right hand showed. His lips were twisting wordlessly; his eyes gleamed down at the cop like the eyes of a cornered rat. His fingers tightened; the gun muzzle rose into line with the policeman's broad tunic. He waited tensely.

Rod Hayle caught up the automatic beside Blossom's writhing body. As the tall cop came thudding past, bound grimly toward sure death, Rod raised the pistol. With a lightning-like sweep of his arm he hit the bluecoat a clean, hard blow on the side of the head.

The man's rush carried him up three steps; then he crashed heavily against the stairs, senseless, limp, but almost completely under cover.

Art Vicar's eyes jerked instantly from what he could see of this slow, fallen enemy to the man of supremely swift reaction time who had taken a commanding hand in the game. Then, as he caught the blue sheen of his own pistol in Hayle's hand he ducked out of sight around the corner.

The train was already pulling out of the station; three passengers who had left it stared irately at Vicar as he plunged through them; leaped the turnstile, caught the iron gate of a moving car and climbed over. The train, gathering momentum, whisked him away.

"Some guys would do anything to save a nickel," one indignant citizen muttered. Then he rounded the turn and stopped at the top of the stairs to stare at two prostrate men—were they dead or drunk?—at the bottom.

5

ONE WAY TO USE A GUN

RODERICK HAYLE HAD turned from the stairs as Vicar vanished. The silent gun in his hand—Art Vicar's automatic—cleared the way for him on Ninth Avenue as effectively as if it were belching lead. He darted toward a tenement house entrance between two store fronts.

Across the street Jud Peltz was just slipping out of the empty chain grocery store. The sound of the shots that had killed Ike Blossom and the cries of the milling throng had cleared the store for him of customers and clerks; Jud had had time, as he had expected, to loot the cash register of its pile of bills. It was not the first time he had worked the one-two robbery in a crowded neighborhood, while acting as a look-out. He sidled away down the street.

Roderick Hayle, in a dark tenement hall, found nothing between him and anonymity on a side street but a single flight of basement stairs and two back fences. He took them at top speed, with Vicar's automatic tucked out of sight.

His own role in the drama had been a matter of seconds only; he did not delay his return to the street or hesitate to pass the outskirts of the crowd around the dead Ike Blossom. The murder weapon was held snugly in the waistband of his trousers.

Ten minutes later he was back on Tenth Avenue. With the aid of one of three skeleton keys that would operate in almost any cheap tenement lock, he opened the door of Jud Peltz's quarters on the fourth floor. He entered briskly, without fear that the flat would be occupied. No crook like Jud would track directly home after a stick-up. Roderick Hayle counted on having at least half an hour of uninterrupted solitude.

He used up only seven minutes in his visit. First he looked around the place. Two bedrooms, one fitted as a sleeping room; the other jammed with pretentious furniture of Grand Rapids and fake antique vintages; a dining room with walnut veneer suite, a living room filled with imposing but uncomfortable chairs. Obviously Jud Peltz had once lived in a larger and more expensive joint but, like all successful crooks, his outlay on lawyers, divvies, rake-offs and blackmail had swallowed most of his income.

Roderick Hayle wiped clean of fingerprints the pistol with which Art Vicar had killed Ike Blossom. He unfastened tacks holding a piece of black material on the bottom of an easy chair, shoved the pistol up among the springs and replaced the tacks, not too carefully. Then he rummaged in Jud Peltz's near-maple desk. Almost at once he found what he sought; a collection of calling cards—fifty each of a dozen sets bearing various names, occupations, and addresses.

Roderick Hayle smiled fleetingly as he ran over them.

"Jud still hopes to break into the confidence racket," he murmured. "He's got the front of a half caste wharf rat, but the boy is ambitious. Or else too yellow to keep on with robbery."

He picked out one of the cards describing its owner as "Winfield M. Bryson, Commission Agent," and put the rest of the Bryson cards back in the desk with the other packs. Then he departed rapidly, leaving no trace of his visit.

ON HIS WAY back to Ike Blossom's pawnshop he dropped in on a Ninth Avenue clothing merchant whose windows blazed on Saturday until midnight with startling lights and bargains. He bought a gray cloth cap, taking care to keep the back of his skull turned from the eager clothier as he switched from his brown felt hat. While in the shop he slipped Jud's professional calling card under the waistband of his trousers. Then, with the felt hat in a paper bag and the cloth cap drawn down securely over the nape of his neck he walked without hesitation toward the scene of Ike Blossom's final contact with crime. That paper bag was the best part of his "disguise," as he knew well.

The avenue was teeming with interested and animated citizens, most of whom had known the dead fence either by his reputation or by his shape. The reserves were out; harassed, sleepy bluecoats attempting to keep the pawnshop, the area around it, and the elevated stairway clear of sightseers for the benefit of the precinct detectives and Headquarters men of the Homicide Squad, including a stenographer, photographers and fingerprint men.

Roderick Hayle pushed his way with steady persistence through the crowd until he was in the second rank of gaping spectators on the sidewalk in front of the shop of the three gilded balls. When the patrolman controlling the section of the ring of pushing citizens went to the aid of a hard-pressed companion, Roderick Hayle surged forward toward the shop front with the other inquisitive ones. Simultaneously he permitted the business card of Winfield M. Bryson, Commission Agent, to slip down inside his trouser leg and thus drop, unseen, to the sidewalk by his feet.

"Get back there!" bawled the reserve an instant later. "Back outta there! Move on, the lot o' youse!"

The front rank of the crowd recoiled as he charged at them; the rear ranks gave ground grudgingly.

Suddenly the red-faced patrolman bent to the sidewalk, jerked a young man's foot aside, and picked up the card of the mythical Mr. Bryson. It was already soiled by the tread of a dozen shoes, but the young policeman handled it as carefully as if it were a new hundred-dollar bill. The card was directly in the line of retreat taken by Vicar from the pawnshop door to the elevated stairs. Turning his back on the crowd the cop rushed toward the pawnshop.

A detective opened the door for him. Roderick Hayle, peering past a dirty derby in front of him, caught sight of this man from the Homicide Squad. It was Detective Sergeant Perrin, and his partner, Sergeant Stock, was close beside him. The Homicide dick accepted the card almost gratefully from the uniformed man.

Apparently Art Vicar had left few tangible clues within.

Roderick Hayle faded away. It had been Perrin and Stock who had headed him toward the death house when he was the Rod. There had been an element of luck in their success, but they were hard-plugging, determined sleuths.

"I can depend on those two," he told himself.

For four blocks Roderick Hayle continued down the

avenue. At that distance all was quiet and normal. Ike Blossom might have been murdered on Mars for all these people dwelling 1,100 feet away cared. It was out of their neighborhood.

In a drug store he found a telephone booth that looked reasonably sound proof and softly called Police Headquarters. He held his watch in his hand as he spoke and watched the movement of the second hand.

"I got some dope for you on the Ike Blossom killing," he said, coarsening his tone as a curt voice announced "Po—lice Headquarters."

"Don't stall me, cop, or I'll hangup."

In surprising short time he was speaking to a Sergeant Grant.

"Get this!" he said, still thickening his utterance a trifle. "Jud Peltz knocked off Ike."

"You think—so—do—you?" drawled Sergeant Grant, lengthily and incredulously. "That's interesting—very interesting. And what—if may ask—makes—you—"

"I'll wait here while you trace the call," Roderick Hayle snapped ironically, still in character. He hung up the receiver and put away his watch. Unostentatiously he slipped out of the store. He heard the bell in an adjoining booth ring furiously even as the door clicked behind him.

"Quick work, Po—lice Headquarters," he applauded.

Circuitously he returned to within a block of the pawnshop. The crowd was thinning now; as an entertainment the fence's murder was failing.

Roderick Hayle lingered in the vicinity with the remaining sightseers. Detectives Perrin and Stock had vanished.

A man with a black bag, obviously the medical examiner,

paid a visit to the pawnshop. That meant that Ike Blossom now lay within, among the pledges and stolen goods of his dual career. The doctor did not stay long. The cause of Ike's death was plain enough.

At last Detectives Stock and Perrin reappeared. They were coming down the avenue. Between them, silent, dead white and stepping jerkily, walked Jud Peltz. The face of the swarthy, narrow-chested little man was an evil mask of thought.

6

THE COPPER SPEAKS

PROMPTLY RODERICK HAYLE moved into the front rank of the inquisitive. The detectives shouldered through the crowd with Peltz's short form securely between them. They halted Peltz an instant at the spot where the young blue-coat had picked up the business card.

"You didn't know that Ike Blossom had in his shop the ice from that Aiken burglary, did you?" Sergeant Perrin asked suddenly. His hand moved casually toward the upper pocket of his waistcoat.

"I don't know nothing about this Blossom," Jud Peltz snarled. "I don't know him an' I've never been near the joint."

"Never?"

"I said 'never'!" Peltz replied emphatically.

"That's too bad," said Sergeant Perrin with heavy sarcasm. He flashed in front of Jud Peltz's dark eyes the soiled card of Winfield M. Bryson. "We figured, Mr. Bryson, when we found this card of yours, that you'd been calling on Ike to-night. But of course we make mistakes, Mr. Bryson."

Jud Peltz stared at the card. The detective replaced it carefully in his pocket.

"And that gun in the seat o' your chair—that'll take some explaining, too, Jud," added Detective Stock genially. "Especially if the marks on the bullets show it was the rod used on Ike. You better quit talking and start hiring a mouth—"

Jud Peltz, licking his lips, spoke suddenly:

"Where'd you find that card?"

The detective's finger stabbed at the sidewalk. "We got you, Jud. Take a tip from me and shut up. You're caught."

"I'm crossed an' framed!" Jud burst out. "Not caught— crossed! And there's only one guy that could ha' done it— the guy that pulled this trick!"

"It might not be the same gun, Jud," Sergeant Perrin suggested.

"I know that gun!" Peltz snapped. "Don't get the idea you're crackin' me, dick. I know that gun. An' I'm opening wide up—myself! I know when to come clean in a hurry. Me take the rap for him? Not a chance! This bird—it ain't the first time he's framed some guy like a picture. I know! There's more'n one sucker up the river that—I c'n tell you plenty. I c'n—"

Gently, without disturbing his flow of words the detectives shepherded him into the pawnshop.

Hayle edged out of the crowd, walked two blocks, bought a roll of strong adhesive tape and hailed a taxi.

"The Hotel Beaulieu, Seventh Avenue near 52nd street," he commanded. "Roll your hoops, cabby; I'm not nervous."

As he rode he tossed his cap out the window and donned his felt hat.

Despite the lateness of the hour the Hotel Beaulieu was busy. The people in the over-ornate lobby and elevators were all Broadway types. Roderick Hayle obtained the number of the suite of A.V. Victor by calling him on the telephone. Mr. "Victor" did not answer, the girl reported.

The rooming clerk obliged him, after a little judicious indecision, by offering a room on the floor above that of Victor's suite. On the ground of nervousness about fire, Roderick Hayle made sure his room was near an emergency exit; he did not doubt that Art Vicar had taken a similar precaution.

He ascended in the elevator to the 17th floor, looked over the location of the floor clerk's desk, and paid off the bellboy at the door of his room. Within two minutes he was slipping down the emergency stairway to the sixteenth floor. In another thirty seconds he was in the sitting room of A.V. Victor's comfortable suite, restoring his homemade key to his pocket. A solitary light burned in the entry to the suite.

AS HE SUSPECTED, Art Vicar had chosen his hideout with suitable provisions for a quiet getaway. One of the two doors of the suite opened upon the main corridor; the other on a side aisle of the big hotel. Near this side passage was the red-lighted emergency exit.

Beginning with a perfunctory tour of the two rooms and a glance into closets and bathroom Roderick Hayle examined the suite. Nothing had been packed for a quick start. There was a litter of personal belongings about, indicating that the hideout had been in active use for some time. He opened the windows and looked out. No fire escape or balcony.

Roderick Hayle switched off all lights save the light in the entry. He sat down in a comfortable chair to wait. His attitude was not too easy, as he glanced at his watch. It was now twenty-four minutes since the babbling, frightened Jud Peltz had entered the pawnshop between the two detectives.

"Will they take him to Headquarters to spill what he knows to the big fellows before they follow up?" he muttered. "Jud knows this hideout of Vicar's."

He set his roll of adhesive tape on the table beside him, slipped his automatic experimentally out of his holster with quick, sure fingers, replaced it and glanced at the door. Minutes dragged slowly by.

A telephone tinkled. It was not the casual hand ringing of a switchboard girl; it was the automatic ring and pause of a Central station.

Roderick Hayle investigated. He switched on the bedroom light. In the room there was, in addition to the hotel installation, another phone—a private line. That was most unusual. He surveyed the telephone tentatively; then, with decision, picked it up.

"Hello?" He spoke in the flat voice of Art Vicar.

"Is that Art?"

Roderick Hayle stiffened abruptly at the sound of the deep authoritative tone of the man on the other end of the wire.

"Art speaking," Hayle replied. "Is that—Copper?" He hesitated.

"You know Copper's voice," said the caller coldly. "You fool, you've done for yourself. Didn't you realize when you framed Jud Peltz that he would squeal his head off on you for this and the Harvey case and everything else?"

Roderick Hayle did not reply, but he looked at his watch

again, frowning. Within twenty-nine minutes of the time
Jud had started to squeal this intangible genius of the telephone knew of it.

"You've got to run, you fool!" the Copper commanded in
cold anger. "There's a general alarm out for you. Get away."

"Can't I bluff it out like—" Roderick Hayle began, allow-
ing incredulity to temper his flat tone.

"Run for it, I said," instructed that icy voice. "You brainless ape; one whisper of corroboration or outside evidence
to prove Peltz's story and you'll be carried out the back
door of the death house while that kid Harvey walks out
the front."

"How did you—"

"Run, blast you!" the Copper broke in. "If I had trusted
your intelligence for an instant I'd be running myself. You
witless hound!"

Of a sudden Roderick Hayle dropped the flat accents of
Art Vicar. He spoke quietly in a voice not too much unlike
his own usual resonant tone:

"You *will* be running yourself—if you can run, Copper.
Your game's up. You've directed your last crime. There's
a man come to town to clean you up-and no telephone
wire is long enough to keep you clear of him. Run or burn,
Copper; that's your choice."

For only an instant was there silence on the wire. Then:

"Who are you?" demanded the Copper guardedly. "If
you think a detective can frighten—"

"I'm no detective, Copper. I'm just a voice on the telephone, like you."

"Ah! Doubtless, then, I address the gentleman who shot
Bells Gwynne and generously gave a dead cop the credit

for that useful deed," said the Copper urbanely. *"The gentle-man with the silver skull!"*

For a moment Roderick Hayle was taken aback by that uncanny knowledge. That squat spy, Lump Engel, had interviewed the dog wagon man, no doubt. With tense lips, he smiled.

"You know a little, but not much, Copper," he said. "I know much—but not all. Keep on trying to save Art Vicar. And if you can't save him—remember what I said: Run or burn!"

He set down the telephone, without awaiting the Copper's acceptance of that challenge. To his ears had come a sound. And it was not from over the telephone wire.

7

A CHILLY TRAP

SOMEONE WAS CAUTIOUSLY inserting a key in the main door of the suite.

Roderick Hayle moved rapidly across the bedroom to the door that opened on the smaller corridor. Then he stopped, with his ear to a panel. Outside that door a foot shuffled on the carpet as if a man was taking his stand by the entrance. There were, then, at least two in this visiting party.

Swiftly he glided to the bedroom window and raised it at the bottom. In an instant he was out on the sill. He shut the window; then opened it a trifle at the top and, flattening himself against the stonework, edged his way a foot along a six-inch ledge that ornamented the towering facade of the building.

The architect had neglected a second ledge for his fingers; he held his position by his feet alone. Every breath he drew pushed his body outward from the sheer wall almost beyond the point of balance.

A night breeze tugged persistently at his coat, as if determined to sweep him off. Then, failing in that, the wind began to chill his body.

Below—for twelve stories—there was nothing. Then

came a setback. Roderick Hayle's eyes noted that with sardonic interest. His body would not strike the street if he fell.

Inside the suite now he could hear vague sounds. Men were talking within. The light in the bedroom threw a steady radiance on the windowsill inches from his feet. Suddenly that illumination was interrupted by a shadow. A man came to the window. Roderick Hayle caught a glimpse of the heavy jowl of Detective Sergeant Perrin as he looked out.

"No exit this way, Ben." The detective's voice filtered faintly through the open window. "We'll wait him out— you here—me down—"

He had gone too far inside the room for Roderick Hayle to hear more, but he had heard more than he wanted to hear. Wavering on that ledge he could not last long. And with the Copper out to warn Art Vicar—

He edged toward the windowsill; sunk his fingers in the side of the embrasure and eased the tense muscles of his feet. Then hearing no sound, he ventured to peer into the room. It was empty. But beyond the open door he could see a section of the sitting room.

Big Ben Stock was shifting the chair in which Roderick Hayle had sat to a position nearer the door.

Hayle listened tensely. Talk—more talk—far too indistinct for him to make out. Then came the click of the door. He had his hands on the window sash when Ben Stock wandered into the room. He paused, frozen, afraid to draw back out of sight lest the movement attract the detective's eyes. But Stock was not interested in windows. He turned the bolt on the bedroom door leading out into the side passage and then vanished into the sitting room again.

For Roderick Hayle time pressed.

"The Copper's warning will reach Vicar unless I get out of here," he whispered. "And if Vicar escapes with that automatic—"

Again he tightened his grip on the window sash. With desperate energy, swaying on his narrow foothold, he struggled with the sash. Finally he started it. Inch by inch he raised it. The night wind blew past him into the room; stirring the curtains. He increased his steady pressure. As he slipped through into the bedroom he heard Ben Stock sneeze; then the detective's chair legs scraped softly on the pile of the carpet as he stood up. The breeze had betrayed him.

Soundlessly Roderick Hayle flung himself across the room. His swift lean hand wrenched at the bolt on the door; then he flung it open and with hunched shoulders leaped out into the corridor.

A REVOLVER BLARED with terrific vehemence through the quiet hall. For a big man Ben Stock moved fast and he shot even faster. But the lead hurtled past Roderick Hayle as he slammed the door. Next instant he was rushing into the cover of the emergency stairs.

He flouted instinct by running up the stairs with feet no noisier than a cat's. He heard Stock fling open the door. He emerged on the seventeenth floor, close to the haven of his newly acquired room. But he did not take cover. That would be defeat. Instead, at a sedate walk, he rounded a corner, proceeded to the nearest bank of elevators and pressed a button.

With a rigid face he waited for a car. Everything depended upon how long Ben Stock would waste searching the staircase.

An elevator stopped. Roderick Hayle sprang into it. Only the gilded operator was on board.

"You're running express," Roderick Hayle assured him, and tickled his ribs with an automatic. "Eyes front."

"Express, s-sir," stammered the man and the car shot downward.

"The minute I step out, slam the door and go up again," Hayle instructed. "Don't stop till you hit the roof."

"The roof, s-s-sir," repeated the frightened operator. His hands shook as he slowed the car at the ground floor.

Roderick Hayle holstered his gun and stepped out into the lobby. The door clanged shut behind him. He caught a glimpse of Sergeant Perrin ambushed behind some palms, watching the Seventh Avenue door. He stepped briskly forward.

Another elevator door opened. Detective Stock bounded out. Roderick Hayle faded behind the reception desk, heading with quickened pace for a side door. Behind came the hoarse shout of Ben Stock.

Instantly he jumped into a run, knocked down a wide-eyed bellboy who lunged at him, and flashed through the side door. Neither Stock nor Perrin dared risk a shot in the crowded lobby. In another five seconds Hayle leaped aboard a cruising taxi, wrenched open the door and slipped into the seat.

The cabby slowed, regarding him with suspicious eyes.

"Keep moving—not too fast yet," Roderick Hayle instructed, glancing backward through the rear window.

Seventh Avenue was jammed with taxis. He could see both the detectives on the sidewalk, shooting questions at pedestrians.

"What is this—the talkies?" growled the driver belligerently, slowing a trifle more.

The doorman of the Beaulieu was pointing toward the cab in which Roderick Hayle had taken refuge. Perrin and Stock jerked out of his limousine a man alighting leisurely in front of the hotel. They leaped on the running board and jabbed their arms simultaneously toward Hayle's taxi.

The liveried chauffeur was staring at them, hands idle on his wheel. Suddenly a taxi cut in in front of the car to discharge passengers.

Roderick Hayle touched the back of the driver's neck with his automatic.

"You're in a silent film, brother," he said crisply. "Round the corner and let her rip."

The man obeyed. His belligerency vanished at the pressure of the gun. He whimpered at the sound of a shot from Perrin's gun.

Roderick Hayle's car reeled around the corner and roared eastward, swaying and bouncing. He sat on the edge of the seat, attentively overlooking the frightened driver's wheelwork. Then he glanced back. The limousine was not yet in sight, but that limousine had had about it a terrible hint of speed and quality.

"Into Sixth Avenue—and then step fast," Hayle commanded. He opened the door and climbed out on the step.

The taxi swung around and screeched to a halt. Roderick Hayle caught the cringing driver by the neck, dragged

him out onto the pavement and slipped in behind the
wheel himself.

"Try an ice wagon!" he snapped at the sprawling taxi
man and sent the car growling into motion again.

The limousine came hurtling into Sixth Avenue; then,
with shrilling tires rounded to follow the cab. The windshield starred near Rod Hayle's head as shots roared out
behind.

"Damn good shooting," he muttered, with gritting teeth,
as he sent the taxi reeling drunkenly around the next corner.

All he had to fight the speed and acceleration of the car
behind was a short wheelbase. He took corners at a speed
that would send a longer car skidding broadside into the
nearest building. Zigzagging, burning rubber, Roderick
Hayle stormed northeastward. With radio patrol cars all
over the city he had to lose that limousine fast. He handled
that car with the sure mastery with which he had once
handled a five-mile-a-minute pursuit plane in the army
air service.

8

"ME!"

BEFORE HAYLE HUMMED into Third Avenue at Sixty-second Street the limousine had faded out. He took care to give the car behind a last glimpse of him turning southward.

Slackening pace, he doubled back to Fifth Avenue, where the taxis were thickest, and drove northward at a sedate twenty-five.

Already, he knew, Station WPEG at Police Headquarters would be droning out the license number and description of this cab—but there were hundreds like this cab in the city and dim-lit license plates are hard to read under the swiftly shifting shadows and radiance of the city streets.

Screened ahead by another taxi bound steadily northward, he chugged up Fifth Avenue and over the 138th Street bridge into the Bronx. Then he drove boldly up the middle of the Grand Concourse.

At Fordham Road he left the Concourse and drove eastward to the Post Road. Then, lurching and bouncing on the cobbles of that broad rough thoroughfare, he continued northward. Once he sighted a radio patrol car, but, hanging carefully behind a Boston bound bus, he passed it in safety.

For an instant his gaze dwelt with something of stern

humor on the lunch wagon where Art Vicar had taken an iron-stone coffee cup on the head.

At the next block he made a turn and ran past the dilapidated filling station in which Vicar kept his handy getaway kit.

His eyes narrowed slightly as he surveyed the place.

It seemed to him that a ray of white light, like a mislaid moonbeam, showed briefly within one dirty window.

Frowning thoughtfully, he drove past the shack. His course took him back to the Post Road. Slowly he swung southward along the highway until he sighted the police patrol car cruising northward. The car was two blocks away.

His foot dropped hard on the throttle. With a whirring, hard-pressed motor, he shot into the nearest side street, almost grazing the blunt front of a truck. Summoning all the speed there was in the cab, he rocketed along the street. His head twisted backward.

The patrol car, after an instant's delay, had followed the speeding cab.

"They waited to check my license plate against the number radioed from Headquarters," Rod Hayle told himself as he slammed northward around the next corner. "They know what they're chasing."

He had a lead of almost three blocks, now, as he spun up the street. He hung onto every yard of it. He drove straight ahead until he saw the car on his trail. Then, with another twist of his wheel that sent the car bouncing and reeling on two wheels, he dry-skidded into the next side street. In fifteen seconds more he was back on the Post Road, once more northward bound. Behind him rose the screech of the police siren, demanding right of way and calling for action from all cops afoot and awheel.

The bullets they fired from the lurching car bored past without damage to cab or driver.

"Ending as it began—by a radio patrol chasing a taxi," Rod muttered, crouching low over the wheel. His right foot was pressing the accelerator flat against the floor boards; the car was doing all it had.

HIS EYES SCANNED the corner of the street of the desolate service station; he hit that turn with a surge of speed that sent the taxi leaping in a broad and terrible slide. Fighting the wheel, he held control and then, with a taut face, turned the cab directly toward the dilapidated shack that was Art Vicar's hideout.

"Here's where you get some corroboration on your squeal, Jud!" he muttered.

The corner of the shack where was Vicar's cache loomed up ahead of his flying wheels. Sternly he held his course to hit the board wall. At the last second he braked enough to save Vicar's hoard from utter demolition. Then he ducked behind the wheel. With crossed arms he shielded his head. The taxi left the street; mounted the sidewalk with a bounce that snapped a spring.

A rending crash split the quiet night as the taxi hit the filling station. The corner of the shack folded up into splintered wreckage. The front end of the taxi crumpled like paper, gushing water and oil. Roderick Hayle's body was slung violently against the instrument board.

Jolted but still conscious, he dragged himself out of the wreckage. For an instant, with quickly clearing brain, he steadied himself beside the demolished cab. His gray eyes surveyed the damage he had wrought. The tire rack in the gaping shack was down; the tires were scattered inside and out. A couple of license plates and Vicar's bag caught his eye.

Nearer and nearer shrilled the siren of the pursuing patrol car.

A man peered out of the ruined building. It was Art Vicar, clad in the suit of dungarees that was part of his getaway outfit. He gripped in his hands the sub-machine gun that had also been in that getaway hoard. The Tommy glittered ominously. Plainly Art Vicar, while in hiding in the shack, had kept it at his side. Neither he nor it had suffered in the crash that had broken open his secret store.

Vicar's head was cocked as, cursing, he listened to the siren.

"Here I am, Art!" Rod Hayle said.

Art Vicar stiffened at the sight of Hayle beside the wrecked cab, his face clearly lighted by the glow from the Post Road.

"You, huh?" he snarled at the man with the silver skull. "You—an' no coffee cups handy! Well, you heel, before them cops—"

He lifted the machine gun to train it upon Roderick Hayle.

Hayle, shifting his body minutely, suddenly was aware that he could not feel the bulge and weight of his automatic in his shoulder holster. The gun had slipped out during the collision.

Roderick Hayle twisted up his face into a semblance of the ravaged and hideous countenance that had been his as the Rod, that ruthless killer. His thin lips curled suddenly.

With a finger he traced the course of the livid scar that once ran from forehead to splayed, broken nose and he spoke in the mocking voice of the killer.

"Me!" he said. "Me, Art! D'you think you can kill *me*, you fool, even with that thing?"

"The Rod!" Art Vicar choked. His eyes bulged. He staggered back, staring, transfixed. "The Rod!"

The shriek of the siren stabbed in their ears as the patrol car swept around the corner into the street.

Rod Hayle had planted a foot on the crumpled fender. With a tremendous leap he was over the hood of the taxi.

Art Vicar jerked up the sub-machine gun, but before the bullets came gushing forth Rod Hayle's flying body had come down on him.

9

THE COLD GUN

ART VICAR AND the machine gun crashed together to the ground. The soaring, bucking gun slipped out of his shaky hands. In an instant he was up again, but in that instant Roderick Hayle had darted on into the blackness of the shack.

The radio car swept up onto the sidewalk near the ruined taxi with that tattoo of machine gun bullets still echoing in the night. The driver caught sight of a man behind the cab—a man who was lifting a Tommy into action.

The cop emptied his revolver without leaving his seat. His partner did the same. Policemen, with only the scanty lead supplied by service revolvers under their trigger fingers, are not fond of sub-machine gun hail. Fast bullets were their one chance.

Art Vicar slumped down on top of his weapon with his chest torn open. His finger slipped from the trigger.

The driver and his companion jumped out of the car, ran around the taxi and plunged at him. But he did not resist— for he was dead. "One down!" muttered the cop.

The driver dropped beside Vicar to make sure of that while his companion moved on toward the gaping black hole in the corner of the shack.

"There was another one," he muttered. "I saw him go in—and there's his gun!"

Crouching under cover, he pushed aside a strange litter of strewn tires, license plates, a razor and a crumpled cigar box from which things like jewels were gushing. He picked up a .45 caliber automatic. But it was cold to his touch, unlike a gun that has been fired or carried against a man's body. With that gun in his hand he ducked back agilely, for the blackness of the shack was menacing.

"Swing that machine gun around, Pete!" he murmured, and then raised his voice. "Come out o' that, you rat!" he shouted into the shack. "In ten seconds we'll slash this joint to ribbons with your own Tommy!"

They waited for an answer, but none came. Suddenly they both turned, for the idling motor of their patrol car had burst into a loud crescendo.

Roderick Hayle, who had darted through the back door and circled the filling station, was in the dark obscurity of the driver's seat.

"Take that .45 automatic to Sergeant Tim Perrin," he called. "It's the one that killed John Bland!"

The policemen rushed toward their car. But the machine leaped ahead with motor revving at full throttle. Before they got back to the machine gun and swung it up, the car was out of range in the distance.

"Stop your cussing, Dan," said the driver to his companion. "If that gat's the one that got Bland and this dead guy's this same Art Vicar that's down in your memo book we ain't done so bad. Not so bad, Dan, if we have lost a flivver. But who that guy—"

In the radio car Roderick Hayle kept his foot down hard on the throttle as he rode away.

But his face was thoughtful, rather than jubilant.

True, a wrong had been righted.

But as he had shot past the junked dump cart in which he had concealed himself at the start of this dance the lights of the patrol car had played briefly upon a man in hiding, a man with an evil, intent face that Roderick Hayle knew of old.

It was the face of Lump Engel, and the face of that squat, bow-backed spying gunman rarely poked itself into danger except when the voice of the Copper commanded. Although the Copper was never more than a voice over a telephone, the Copper's eyes saw much.

How much? Roderick Hayle could not tell, but he knew he had found Vicar and won the game only by scant seconds. Lump Engel was a messenger of the Copper as well as one pair of his many eyes.

IN THE UNFAMILIAR cell in the "dance hall," just outside the Sing Sing death chamber door, to which he had been transferred according to routine on the morning of the day of his execution, Vincent Harvey struggled with the sketch of the bridge which never would be built. He worked grimly, with compressed lips. He had eleven hours to live, and strangely enough, the time was dragging.

When, not long before noon the warden came to the door of his cell, Harvey did not spring to his feet. He nodded, set down his drawing board and slowly stood up. There was no hope in his eyes—merely a resignation that was not pleasant in so young a face.

"How are you?" asked the warden anxiously.

Vincent Harvey forced a painful smile.

"All right—so far," he said steadily.

The warden did not smile at that grisly jest.

"You can stand some good news, then," he said quietly. "Something has happened in New York. In fact, a lot has happened, including some rather inexplicably fortunate events. A cheap crook named Peltz squealed on that fellow Vicar who testified against you at your trial. Peltz accused Vicar and Rod Hayle, who has been dead some time, of Bland's murder."

Vincent Harvey nodded. "Naturally I always thought Vicar was guilty," he said hoarsely. "I—I was in a position to know that his testimony was utterly false."

"But Peltz's accusation was not enough. He charged Vicar with other crimes and actually established his own innocence of the murder of a fence named Blossom on Saturday night by confessing a store robbery that occurred simultaneously. All that was not enough to help you, of course, but it set the police after Vicar."

"Go on!" muttered Harvey.

"Art Vicar was killed in a hideout in the Bronx. By a strange chance they found in the place, within a few feet of Vicar's dead hand, the very gun with which Bland was murdered. Undoubtedly the missing gun!"

"And that means—that—that—"

"There are a few things about the affair that not even the police seem to understand. But the case against you has been ripped to shreds."

Vincent Harvey sank onto the bunk, staring at the sketch of his bridge. He hardly heard the warden's voice:

"No papers have come through yet. But I've received a

telephone order from Albany staying the execution. You'll be turning your back on—that door, Harvey—instead of going through it."

RODERICK HAYLE STEPPED into a telephone booth—the double door variety—set his brown felt hat more firmly back on his head and called the office of Dr. John Arnold, the celebrated brain surgeon.

Dr. Arnold answered himself, for the number Hayle called was a private wire.

"This is—Silver-Skull," said Roderick Hayle briskly to the man whose skill had altered both his cranium and brain. "Doctor, would you mind destroying that sealed envelope I mailed you the other day for use should Vincent Harvey not be reprieved—or in the event that I—ah—died suddenly? The envelope contained a confession of my identity and of my share in the Bland murder."

"You do not intend, then, to sacrifice yourself in the death chair for crimes you committed when not responsible?" Dr. Arnold inquired mildly.

"Since Vincent Harvey is not to die I'll hang on a bit longer myself," Roderick Hayle replied.

"I have a few more things like this Vicar job to live for. There's one in particular that would be a useful bit of work."

"What is that?"

"This gentleman with the voice—Copper almost managed to warn Vicar in time," Hayle explained. "Before I can hope to work unimpeded, Copper and I must get together. We've had dealings before, he and I, but these dealings are going to be different."

A CLUE TO THE COPPER

*The Half-Drowned Man That He Pulled from
the Little Connecticut Bay Was but the Prologue
to the Drama of Hate That Silver Skull Faced
in His Search for an Underworld Fiend*

1

THE DESERTED SEAPLANE

CAPTAIN RODERICK HAYLE, formerly of the U.S. Air Service, but more recently known to an unselect few as Silver Skull, looked hard toward the gray, obsolete flying boat moored out in the muddy little Connecticut bay. He turned to the man beside him.

"I can't see anybody aboard her now," he said curtly to the owner of the oyster dock on which he stood.

"Can't help it," said the old oysterman with Yankee doggedness. "This jailbird, Will Sheppard, who owns her, he took out a customer in a rowboat no more'n three minutes ago. An'—hum!"

He cackled shrilly, pointing a gnarled finger. "That passenger must have changed his mind right quick about flyin'. Look! There he goes in the boat—across the bay!"

With tightening lips and narrowed eyes Roderick Hayle stared at the rowboat. The small man in it was rowing smoothly and strongly toward the opposite shore, aided by the blasts of a blusterous spring northeaster. Just one man—not two. And there was nobody aboard that open cockpit flying boat, either.

In quick decision he jumped aboard the dirty little oyster boat.

*As Hayle flung his burden
on board the plane, the cop's
whistle was reinforced by shots*

"One dollar to take me out," he said, and started the motor himself with practiced hands.

The owner stood, arms akimbo and lips framing crabbed remonstrance. But he encountered just then the full force of the slate gray eyes of Roderick Hayle. They had fire in their depths. With feverish haste he scrambled aboard. He was just in time, for Hayle was already casting off the lines.

The oyster boat had no flair for speed, but Roderick Hayle saw that it did its best. In two minutes it was nearing the seaplane, with the owner at the wheel and Roderick Hayle standing in the bow.

Suddenly he bent forward, eyes on the surface of the bay just ahead.

"Cut her down!" he shouted to the boatman and flung himself half over the gunwale. One long thin arm directed the course of the sluggish craft, the other trailed over the water.

The boatman, busy as he was, gawked in jaw-sagging stupefaction at the back of the head of this positive young fellow who had so curtly commandeered his boat. There showed under the oversize brown hat a tiny crescent of shining silver—as if part of his skull bone had been replaced by metal. Partly hidden under the longish, prematurely gray hair of this strange young man, it gave the boatman a turn.

But in another instant he almost forgot his turn, for the young man, with more power than his lean arms suggested, was dragging out of the water the body of a thin little man.

"It's Sheppard—the flyin' man!" he gasped.

With swift fingers Roderick Hayle stripped the dripping emaciated figure of a shabby leather jacket and a blackened, ancient helmet. He thrust his arms under Sheppard's middle and held him, with gaunt head dangling, while water poured out of his lungs. Then, briefly, he inspected a lump on the side of the aviator's head.

"Just a crack on the head and a drink of salt water," Roderick Hayle diagnosed. "He'll be coming to in no time. Now—"

"He wouldn't be comin' to if my boat hadn't got to him right smart," said the oysterman emphatically.

But Roderick Hayle was looking now toward the rowboat, which was close to the low and marshy shore at a place where no houses lined the bank. The oarsman was short, slender, and clad in gray.

"That passenger must have seen him fall off the wing, hit his head and sink," he asserted, his slaty eyes boring in the faded blue orbs of the oysterman. "Then he got panicky and rowed ashore, to get help."

"I reckon!" snarled the oysterman, without much interest. "Just my darn luck to rescue a man without a mite o' money to recompense me! This Sheppard, he's been around here three days and he ain't got a dime to—"

"You can land me on that ruined pier over there," Roderick Hayle broke in brusquely. "I'll go after that fellow and tell him Sheppard's all right, so he won't run a mile and rouse the village. You look after Sheppard."

"ALL RIGHT, BUT I'd ought to get paid more for my trouble," complained the old man. Hastily he turned the wheel as Roderick Hayle started toward him. The boat thrust sluggishly through the thick water.

Sheppard's passenger was ashore now, and moving with more effort than speed through the high grass and mud of the marsh.

As they neared the wharf Roderick Hayle thrust a five-dollar bill from his meager roll into the eager hand of the oysterman.

"Don't let him leave your place till he's feeling fit," he said, and scrambled up on the bow of the motorboat. With a quick bunching of his muscles he sprang across the watery gap to the wharf. Side-stepping a gaping hole, he sprinted down the tottering, treacherous structure.

At the end he came to ground a little firmer than the marsh through which the passenger had made his way. The man was out of sight, now, but Roderick Hayle had marked his course carefully and he struck out on a converging one. The ground rose, and became a scrubby little pine wood. With legs pumping like connecting rods the man with the silver disk in his head plunged on headlong, varying his pace only to duck or dodge as the trees grew thicker.

Suddenly he struck a path and, following it in a burst of

speed, caught sight of a dirt road ahead. To his ears, as he covered those last few yards, came the rasp of a car accelerating swiftly in low.

He leaped the ditch and stood in the road, facing that sound. From his shoulder holster he jerked out a business-like automatic. The next instant a car came screaming toward him around a turn.

It was a gray touring car in no way unusual looking, save that the top was down. And, sitting next to the driver, was a slim, sandy-haired gentleman in gray tweed. Roderick Hayle recognized him instantly by one unchanged characteristic. On his lips was a smile—a smile without reason, perpetual, masking his mood and thoughts as no blankness could mask.

"Fingy Catlin!" he grunted. He raised his gun. By gesture and voice he commanded the machine to halt.

The car leaped ahead, and the smiling one dug for a gun with smooth swiftness.

Hayle fired instantly, holding his place in the middle of the road. His bullet starred the windshield, in line with the driver's shoulder. But the car roared on—straight for him, despite the bullets he sent blaring at it with steady aim.

At the last instant, with an agile backward spring, he saved himself from its remorseless thrust. Even as he tottered into the ditch he finished the clip by snap-shooting at the nearest tire. The whirring rubber target shot past as he thudded into the muddy bottom of the trench. The brown mud seemed to explode into minute craters in the side of the ditch as he raised his head, and his ears rang with the diminishing roar of the smiling gentleman's gun. The smile was a snarl of blood lust now as the man hung over the side of the disappearing car, firing with furious speed. Only the roughness of the road on which the car was bounding saved Roderick Hayle from death. It was good shooting. But in no time that grinning peril and the car were gone.

Slipping another clip into his gun, Roderick Hayle climbed up onto the road again. His eyes dropped to one rut. There lay a chunk of twisted metal that once had been a steel-jacketed bullet.

"Bullet-proof windshield," he murmured. "That's bad! Bad for Will Sheppard. It means Fingy Catlin's not trying a casual murder on his own. He's got backing—and there's only one who would back Fingy to get Will Sheppard. Only one!"

At a dog trot he started after the car. It was a hundred to one that he had missed that tire but even that chance must not be overlooked. If he had even nicked the rubber it might blow out. With iron determination, eyes on the dirt road, he followed.

2

SILVER SKULL'S LIST

RODERICK HAYLE DREW out of his breast pocket a folded sheet of paper. Quietly, with a thin hand, he placed the sheet on the desk of Dr. John Arnold.

"There's a man on that list whom I've moved to the top—to act on before he dies," he said crisply.

The famous brain surgeon scanned the sheet with obvious foreboding. Some on that list were dead of violence—murdered men or suicides. Others on it might have accounted themselves lucky if they had died, but they still hung on, struggling to repair wrecked lives.

Even the most fortunate had been grievously harmed by the tall grim young man at Dr. Arnold's shoulder.

Strangely, all now alive in that company of grief believed that the malefactor who had wronged them was dead. The end of Captain Roderick Hayle, formerly of the Air Service, more lately Rod Hayle of the underworld, had been proclaimed on the front page of every newspaper in the country.

Dr. Arnold, who had reason to know how Roderick Hayle had happened to survive, frowned in unease at that list.

"You mean—another of these men is under sentence of death?" he asked.

Roderick Hayle nodded slowly. "Under sentence of death—but not by the state," he said. "Unless I am mistaken this man is under sentence of death by the Copper."

At the mention of that elusive and terrible individual, the brain behind those crimes in which Roderick Hayle had been the daring and ruthless hand, Dr. Arnold's unrest grew acute. He stood up, the better to confront this taut-faced young man who had once been his unwilling patient.

"If you had a chance against the Copper I would say nothing," the surgeon said. "But you cannot fight an individual whose person, creatures, powers, are all unknown to you. You should not invite annihilation at his hands.

"I tell you that you are morally guiltless of the deeds, black as they are, that you committed from the time of your airplane crash to the time of my operation to relieve the pressure upon your brain."

His voice became thin and small in its extreme urgency. "I tell you this though you murdered my own son, Hayle. I tell you this as a scientist, knowing positively your condition during your career in the underworld."

The face of Roderick Hayle remained implacable, though his voice shook a trifle as he replied:

"And I must say to you, doctor, that in spite of my deep gratitude and my respect for your wisdom, I must use my life for one purpose. That is to repair in some part the ruin I have brought to many people."

With a sigh Dr. Arnold sat down at his desk.

"If you should by chance escape the Copper there remains the practical certainty that the police will identify you as an escaped prisoner condemned to the electric chair," he warned. "Though I altered your face and destroyed the pattern of your finger prints you are far from safe."

"I, Simon Stark to the world at large, want to live, and strive to live," said Silver Skull. "I promise you that I will be as cautious—"

"Yes?" said the doctor more hopefully when the young man paused.

"As cautious as my purpose permits," Roderick Hayle concluded inflexibly.

"I cannot move you," murmured the surgeon, picking up the list once more. "After all, you have saved an innocent man from execution. Perhaps I should accept your Quixotism with resignation.

"Who is this unfortunate whom you suspect the Copper would kill? And why?"

"There's his name. Will Sheppard, formerly chief flying executive of the Airspeed Corporation, easily the largest commercial aviation outfit in the world.

"Sheppard was the guiding spirit—the hard working inspiration of flying in this country—before the Copper called me on the telephone one day and, together with Fingy Catlin, we blasted the man's career."

"And what makes you—"

"ONLY THIS," SAID Roderick Hayle, and laid upon the desk a brief clipping from a newspaper.

WILL SHEPPARD ESCAPES DEATH
BY SCANT MARGIN
Picked Up Unconscious in Sound; He Blames Propeller.

Will Sheppard, who until two years ago was Airspeed Corporation's flying ace, was picked up unconscious yesterday afternoon in Long Island Sound near Westport, Conn., by an oyster fisherman.

Although once a big shot in aviation, Sheppard now is a barnstormer, carrying such passengers as he can induce to take a chance in an old flying boat. He is both pilot and mechanic of this craft, in which he roams over the Sound and Jamaica Bay. He is said to make his home in an old houseboat located somewhere in the latter body of water.

According to Dave Price, skipper of the oyster boat, he sighted the body of Sheppard, which was buoyed up by air in his flying suit, floating a quarter of a mile off shore. He dragged Sheppard into his boat and by prompt treatment managed to revive him.

Sheppard, who had a gash on his head, came to after half an hour, but his account of what had happened to him was vague.

According to Captain Price, Sheppard thanked him warmly, promised him a reward if times got better, and attributed his trouble to the propeller of the flying boat.

"Call it a balky prop that back-fired and cracked me on the head," he said to the oyster skipper. "That's as good a yarn as any, isn't it?"

He denied that he had been drinking.

Although Will Sheppard was regarded as easily the most promising young man in the rapidly developing commercial aviation business, he is said to have gone downhill fast since he was released from jail. A jury disagreed in his trial on a charge of complicity in murder and the looting of a consignment of cash carried by one of the Airspeed Corporation's transcontinental ships.

Sheppard, it may be recalled, volunteered to pilot through a threatening blizzard an Airspeed monoplane, flying the regular route from Chicago to New York, with only two passengers on board. Also in the machine was a little brown suitcase, locked in the mail compartment, containing a quarter of a million in bills of large denomination.

It was Sheppard's contention that over the Alleghanies the General Manager's blue plane ranged alongside his. The pilot of this plane, he maintained, waved him down to a small emergency field in a wild section of the mountains. There thugs waited to rob the ship. One of the two passengers was killed and the other wounded.

Following the disagreement of the jury Sheppard was released, but he lost his job and has been unable to obtain another. Some time ago he managed to get hold of the old flying boat and since then has been barnstorming on his own.

Dr. Arnold handed the clipping back to Roderick Hayle. "I fail to see anything suspicious in that," he said. "The inference is that the man was drunk and tumbled overboard—or perhaps hurt himself while trying to start his propeller."

Roderick Hayle nodded. "That's the inference," he agreed. "And fortunately that old oyster pirate knows how to grab the limelight to the exclusion of everyone else. Two other characters were on the stage, doctor, one Fingy Catlin and myself."

"You? What were you—"

"As Simon Stark, a plain citizen desirous of taking a

flight, I was planning to look over what is left of the once useful Will Sheppard."

"What made you desert the sequence of your list?"

Roderick Hayle picked up his hat. "I learned that a certain distant link I have with the Copper—a stupid thug named Lump Engel who obeys without asking questions or making deductions—was spending a few of these cold spring days down in dismal, shutdown Rockaway. Sheppard's retreat is somewhere down there."

"But why should the Copper or this man Catlin be interested any longer in Sheppard?"

"There is one possible explanation," Roderick Hayle assured the surgeon. "Just suppose Sheppard was no flying drunk; suppose he'd been digging into the crime that had ruined him and had uncovered some stimulating clues to the actual perpetrators of that crime. He may even have a clue to the Copper! How long after the Copper heard that do you suppose Sheppard would live?"

"But is it likely that the Copper would keep track for all these months of the activities of a mere victim like Sheppard?"

Roderick Hayle nodded gravely. "It is likely. Don't ask me how—but the Copper knows these things."

Dr. Arnold stared doubtfully at the breast pocket in which Roderick Hayle had placed the newspaper clipping.

"Remember this," he warned. "Though the Copper is not aware that you are Roderick Hayle he knows that a gentleman with a silver plate in his skull is interfering with his plans. And remember, Hayle—I mean Simon Stark— the Copper is still only a disembodied voice over the telephone—a mere evil spirit—to you."

"An evil spirit," repeated Roderick Hayle bitterly, his fingers tight on the door handle. "Am I likely to forget that, doctor? I who was once literally possessed by that devil?"

The old surgeon did not reply.

"An evil spirit," Roderick Hayle said once more. "But that evil spirit may have his familiar—a crook I have seen in flesh and blood—perhaps Fingy Catlin, doctor.

"And through him perhaps I can get to his master. Certainly I must watch and stand behind Will Sheppard—not only for his sake but for my own purpose."

"It is a tenuous thread," murmured the doctor.

"I'd follow a spider's filament—if I thought there was a chance it led the right way."

Roderick Hayle's face was sombre as Huong, the servant and laboratory assistant of the surgeon, silently attended him to the outer door of the Park Avenue apartment.

3

TRAILED!

RODERICK HAYLE, HIS back to the flimsy wooden fence, raked the street of tawdry amusement enterprises with gray eyes as wary as a raiding hawk's.

On that fading, bleak afternoon the place seemed as deserted as it deserved to be. It would require a warm sun, gallons of cheap and lurid paint and the strident voices of many barkers to draw people to that particularly unpleasing part of the long Rockaway peninsula.

Nevertheless Roderick Hayle knew it was not as devoid of humanity as it appeared. With a gesture that was becoming habitual he drew his brown felt hat back on his head. Worn like that it covered completely the gleaming silver disk.

Turning, he reached with his long spare arms to the top of the fence. Swiftly he pulled his gaunt body up until he could look over the barrier.

Within, in the center of a small plot, stood a half burned, dilapidated wreck of a tower, perhaps fifty feet high. Some winter fire had badly damaged the rounded structure. Across the front of the blackened framework, an electric sign from which all electric bulbs were gone proclaimed it "The Tower of Thrills." Plainly enough the thrills were derived from the descent of a concave spiral slide, badly damaged, which wound around the outside of the curving framework, terminating in a straight chute at the ground level. Roderick Hayle eyed the sad tower with strange tensity.

For just an instant there was revealed at one of the windows halfway up the figure of Lump Engel. A bowbacked, thick-chested fellow with flat, unlovely features, he drifted past the opening like a wraith. Over his fawncolored, vivid coat was slung a large leather case for binoculars. A moment later the man's body showed fleetingly at a higher window. He was ascending the stairs within the tower, keeping close to the inner wall of the winding staircase.

Roderick Hayle's eyes had not moved a fraction of an inch above the fence. Now, as Lump's curving progress took him to the other side of the tower, he slipped over the fence as lithely as if there were no weight at all to his attenuated body. He glided across the fenced enclosure to the base of the tower on noiseless feet.

The entrance to the shaky structure had been boarded up, but several planks pried away at the bottom revealed how Lump Engel had crawled in. Swiftly Roderick Hayle dropped to his knees and crept in with the most painstaking caution. Any hint that Silver Skull was about would be quite enough to ruin this game.

He found himself at the bottom of the charred, steep winding stairs. At twice the speed that Lump Engel was making but with no more noise Roderick Hayle moved toward the top of the tower. Only near the upper reaches, where the tower was a mere shell of half burned beams, did he slow his pace. Then, keeping close to the staircase-well, he climbed the last few steps like a shadow. With infinite caution he raised his head to the level of the platform at the top.

In one of the embrasures of the parapet, looking toward the many-islanded expanse of Jamaica Bay, Lump Engel was kneeling. His binoculars were levelled toward the bay and his flat, unpleasant countenance was further disfigured by a scowl of concentration.

At once Hayle withdrew. He crept down the stairs until their curving course brought him, ten feet below, to a window looking out in the same direction in which the gunman above was staring.

Through this, though with an ear alert for any movement of the man above, Roderick Hayle looked with a far sighted eye. The detail of a landscape was an easy matter for him to absorb, for his eyes had been trained by many a hundred hours in the air. Upon one thing did his gaze finally come to rest. His ordinarily expressionless countenance showed a tinge of speculation, almost of wonder, as he looked.

The bay was a hodge podge of water, grassy islands, shacks upon stilts over shallows and shacks planted upon brief stretches of sand, a few bungalows of less poverty stricken aspect, and houseboats and other craft with an air of weary stolidity about them, as if they had finally cast anchor till worm and weather destroyed them. Many of these, indeed, were high and dry on beaches, far above their familiar element, as if their owners doubted their ability ever again to float.

The thing that Roderick Hayle was gazing at was what aviators call a wind sock, a wind direction indicator, floating from a stubby mast. The pole was planted on an unpainted, shattered wreck of a houseboat. It lay aslant on the sand on a point of land projecting into the bay.

"THAT'S WHAT LUMP is watching—that houseboat," Roderick Hayle muttered with conviction. "There's Will Sheppard's refuge—a wind sock flying over a wrecked hovel. Can't see any flying boat. Was Lump on the look-out for that?"

He nodded slowly, still with his eyes upon that forlorn indicator of the wind. "It's no coincidence," he decided. "I'd better hurry."

He swung away from the window, facing toward the downward slant of the stairs. And suddenly his thin body stiffened.

A man was standing three steps below him on the stairs. He had been trailed!

The man was a big fellow, with a chest like a hogshead and a face like a purple moon. His huge fleshy lips drooped slackly but he fingered with accustomed ease a nickel-plated .38 calibre revolver. The muzzle was levelled steadily at Roderick Hayle's stomach, at more than the reach of Hayle's arm from its target. A grin twisted the full-blooded lips as Hayle stood tautly motionless.

With leisurely confidence the man raised his head to hail Lump Engel on the parapet above. His eyes merely flickered away in a momentary instinctive glance upward. But in that instant Roderick Hayle acted.

Under the menace of the steady revolver there was just one thing that Hayle could do. But he did that thing well. With utter disregard of self he launched his thin body at the man three steps below.

The fellow had to choose instantly between shooting and catching at something to brace himself against the lunge of the hurtling body. He tried to save himself.

Even as his hands closed on a blackened beam Roderick Hayle thudded down on him. The big thug went backward down the stairs, with Hayle jammed against his shoulders. For a dozen feet they rolled. Nails projecting from the half-burned woodwork took toll of their flesh.

All at once one of the man's clutching arms hooked into a flimsy rail guarding the inner well.

Gripping that, he halted his fall and jerked up his gun. His torn face was twisted with berserk rage; his blood-blinded eyes were blinking desperately.

Roderick Hayle, on his knees, inches away, lunged desperately at the man again. His right fist swung upward toward the out-thrust, belligerent jaw below that red and purple face.

The fist landed squarely; it seemed to drive backward the whole bulk of the man. The rails of the inner well creaked ominously; then, like a wave, the railing bent inward for twenty feet and broke suddenly away.

The gunman, with his pistol still unfired, plunged down the well. The yell of fear that came shrilling from his throat ended abruptly as his body smashed upon the concrete foundation at the base of the tower. Just that one sullen thud, amidst the crackling of the fallen railing. Then complete silence.

Hayle, recoiling from the edge of the well, leaped toward the nearest window. He wasted not an instant upon the fallen man; his whole brain focused, as one enemy hurtled downward, upon Lump Engel above. He must not be seen now.

He leaped to the windowsill, seeking cover that the stairs did not offer. His eyes fell upon the curving, high-sided trough provided for sliding merrymakers. Flinging himself down in it, he clutched at a joint in the planking where the flames had burned through the wood.

Already Lump Engel's feet were pounding across the platform above to the top of the stairs. Hayle, silent and still, marked the pause as the man peered down; then heard his feet descending. He clattered past the window outside which Roderick Hayle lay in the trough. Immediately Hayle, gripping the sides of the steep incline, lowered himself at grievous cost to his skin and clothes down the charred slide. As long as he kept a few feet above Engel he could not be seen and Engel's own feet made more than enough noise to blanket his movements.

Near the bottom Roderick Hayle slipped once more back into the tower through a window. He stared over the railing into the inner well. A little trickle of blood from a wound ripped by a nail trickled down his arm and dripped steadily on a stair tread.

4

THE COPPER'S DEMAND

LUMP ENGEL STOOD below, in the litter of broken palings, with the limp body of the fallen man at his feet. With the toe of one shoe Lump Engel moved the bleeding head. The neck was horribly twisted.

Lump spoke to the corpse mockingly, as if it were still a living man.

"Tailin' me, huh, Sammy? I knew the Copper kept checked on all us guys, but I didn't think he'd use a clumsy heel like you ta do it. You must ha' been stewed to the gizzard, Sammy, fallin' through the rail like that."

He gave vent to a hoarse cackle of mirth. "If ya'd landed on yer head, Sammy, ya'd have been jake, but yer neck must be tender as a baby's. Tough break, Sammy, tough break."

He squatted beside the body, jerked the revolver out of the clutch of the dead fingers and detached from under the shoulder a holster in which it had been carried. Then, methodically, Lump went through the dead man's pockets, taking even his cigarettes.

"I'll leave ya fifteen cents an' a box o' matches, Sammy," he muttered, straightening up. "Where you're gone you don't need no price of admission—it's free."

After a sharp inspection of the deserted grounds inside

the concession he wormed his way out under the boarded up doorway of the tower. Then came the thud of his heels as he kicked the boards back into place.

Roderick Hayle crouched in the embrasure of a window and watched the bow-backed, furtive little thug scale the fence. Then he swung himself out onto the slide and dropped to the ground. He was not ninety seconds behind Lump Engel in climbing over the fence.

At the first corner Lump paused, looked around and plainly saw nobody. Quickly he drew out from under his coat the late Sammy's revolver and holster and poked them down into the sewer. Then he straightened up, looked at his watch, and moved on, his attitude toward the world no longer wary and surreptitious.

When Sammy's body turned up the police would be far less interested in it than they would have been if a revolver were found in the stiffened fingers. A dead hobo doesn't count.

Until Lump passed out of the desolate region of amusement concessions, Roderick Hayle made it a long tail. There was danger of losing his man but that could not be helped. He must not be seen. That was vital. Only when Lump came to a main street in which signs of life were apparent and the sidewalks were busy did Silver Skull venture to close up a trifle.

Lump Engel looked at his watch again and quickened his pace. Roderick Hayle's long, thin legs spurned the pavement in swift, space-consuming strides when Lump turned into a small stationery store.

Lump was already out of sight in a telephone booth in the back of the store when Roderick Hayle entered.

Behind the counter stood a fat man with a head like a cone cut off at the top.

Fleetingly Roderick Hayle flung back his coat. His was now the brusque manner of authority. Although there was no shield to be seen pinned to the waistcoat beneath the coat the stout man's belated eyes grew big, nevertheless. Hayle leaned over the counter, punched himself in the chest and spoke softly, close to the storekeeper's flaring ear.

"Detective Sergeant Matthew Quinn. I want you to get on another telephone somewhere and ask Central what number the man in that booth is calling and where it's located."

"But the store—" protested the man with the tapering head feebly.

"I'll look after the shop," Roderick Hayle assured him grimly. His right hand moved ominously toward his hip pocket. "You're safer out o' here, anyhow."

"Sergeant, I'm goin' fast!" the fat storekeeper said fervently. He whisked to the door as lithely as a ballet dancer and vanished.

Quietly Roderick Hayle moved toward the telephone booth. He stopped for a moment and laid his ear against the side of it.

Lump Engel was speaking in a mere husky murmur. It was impossible to make out more than a word here and there, but Hayle heard the name Sammy and grasped that the spy was recounting the gunman's passing and emphasizing the fact that he, Lump, had played no part in it save that of the sorrowing friend.

While Hayle listened, one of his hands crept toward the door of the booth and the other toward his left armpit.

Engel's voice muttered on into the receiver and once

Roderick Hayle's lips tightened as he caught the word "plane." Then, abruptly, Lump ceased to speak into the receiver. He listened a moment and then spoke more plainly.

"Huh?" he said. "Ya want me to come back to town?"

Of a sudden Roderick Hayle's thin finger tapped loudly and imperatively upon the glass panel of the booth door. His body was out of sight at the side of the booth, but there was nothing surreptitious about that tapping finger.

"Wait a second, boss," Lump said.

HE OPENED THE door and stuck out his flat, belligerent countenance. His lips were framing a blasphemous remonstrance.

Hayle's automatic cracked him neatly on top of the head. Hayle's other hand guarded his face from Engel's black eyes, but it was a needless precaution. Lump Engel was out.

Instantaneously, before Lump could slump, Hayle seized him by the shoulders. He thrust him back into the booth and stepped in with him. Then he let Lump sag to the floor.

Without haste he picked up the telephone receiver.

"Go ahead, boss," he muttered hoarsely. "Some guy couldn't wait but I fixed 'm."

"Come back to town," said the man at the other end in a crisp, cold voice. "Show yourself to the cops or plant an alibi. I'm closing this—both ends."

Roderick Hayle's keen gray eyes narrowed at the sound of that voice. He knew it damnably well, though never had he seen its owner. It was the voice of the Copper.

"Back t' town, boss?" he repeated.

"Don't Fingy need no help to—"

"Forget that name, you clod!" said the Copper sharply. "To town—at once. You'll hear from me when I want you again." The transmitter clicked in Roderick Hayle's ear as his invisible enemy disconnected.

Roderick Hayle hung up. He stepped out of the booth, eyes alert.

He dragged Lump's limp figure half out of the booth, screening it with his own body, as with a half smile, he bent over it. As rapidly as Lump had frisked Sammy, a few minutes before, Roderick Hayle searched Lump Engel.

"It's only right," he murmured sardonically as he slipped Lump's roll into his own almost empty pocket. "Lump would expect a sock-and-frisk man to take everything but his shirt—and his gun. I wouldn't want him to think this tap on the skull had anything to do with the Copper's private business."

He looked up hastily. The fat storekeeper's nose was pressed whitely against the glass of the front door. The man himself was poised for instant flight as he peered in with timorous, bulging eyes.

Roderick Hayle pushed Lump Engel back into the booth and shut the door. Then he advanced into the better lighted front of the store.

The storekeeper saw him and entered immediately.

"I got it the number, sergeant!" he whispered proudly, and handed Hayle a scrawl on a paper. "It's a cigar store, Central says, an' not four blocks from police hetquarters on Centre Street. Iss— Iss he still telephoning?"

Roderick Hayle nodded, staring in some disappointment at the telephone number. Doubtless just a joint where anyone might receive a call. But it might help—possibly. He turned his eyes to the door and slantingly caught sight of a bluecoat advancing briskly up the street.

"And, too, I got it a cop coming to help you," the store-keeper with the truncated head announced. "While I was in Bennie's shop I sent his boy down to the lunch—"

Roderick Hayle seized the shopkeeper by both shoulders, whirled him toward the door and started him moving with a shove.

"Good work!" he applauded. "But get down there on the run and tell the cop to hurry! Quick! Make him come on the jump! Get it?"

"I got it!" The man was off. He began yelling to the policeman just outside the door.

In some haste Roderick Hayle swung toward the back of the store. He rushed past the telephone booth, where Lump Engel still slept with his illegal automatic in his coat pocket.

In the back of the store were living quarters, fortunately empty. Hayle went through the crowded ranks of cheap, over-ornate furniture like a bullet through a matchbox, and found the back door by crashing against it.

Jerking it open he emerged into a squalid back yard. His eyes raked it in one sweep. Catching up a packing box, he flung it into position against the low back fence; then scaled the side fence.

A moment later he was hurrying by a narrow alley back to the street on which the store fronted. There he made one of scores already converging, as if by instinct upon the stationery store in which something unusual was happening. He wasted little time in making his departure, though it was the length of his stride rather than any obvious haste that gave him speed.

5

DANGEROUS VISITORS

FIFTEEN MINUTES LATER Roderick Hayle's feet were wet and his old blue serge suit already torn, showed further damage from climbing fences designed to prevent trespassers from reaching the delights of the Bay. He had held almost a compass course for the stranded houseboat with the wind sock flying from the stubby mast above it. Nobody had challenged him, for dwellers near the bay were still scarce.

Now he was close to that poverty-stricken refuge of Will Sheppard, who, two short years before, had been the chief flying executive of the Airspeed Corporation.

He walked out on a sandy point and quietly climbed from the sand bar up onto the slanting deck of the houseboat. One look at that gaping deck told him that this craft would never float again though, conceivably, the flimsy, crazy house built on it might blow away on the slightest encouragement.

For a moment he stood on that weathered deck, scanning the house and the sky with the puffy white clouds of a northwesterly breeze scudding briskly across it.

There was within sight no flying boat; no hum of a motor reached his ear.

Satisfied of that, Roderick Hayle walked to the door of the houseboat, struck it with his fist by way of knocking, and walked into the shack when the door swung on sagging hinges.

A small man with a wry neck looked up from a rusty coal stove on which he was frying bacon.

"Mr. Sheppard in?" Hayle asked mildly.

"What the hell do you want?" the cook demanded, with overlarge mouth sagging at the sight of the intruder. He winked his eyes, reddened by the smoke that rose from the stove and swirled through a skylight in the roof. "Get to hell out o' here!"

"You Sheppard's dogrobber?" Roderick Hayle inquired, casually dropping down on a faded camp chair near the stove.

"I ain't been paid so long I'm just about his pardner," retorted the man with the wry neck. "Also my name's Mister Pond to housebreakers, in case you want to know."

"When's Sheppard due back?"

"About any time he damn well feels like it, by his reckoning," retorted Mr. Pond. He stirred the hissing bacon vigorously, but his red-rimmed, suspicious eyes never left his visitor. "But me, I eat when it's time to eat, regardless."

Roderick Hayle drew out a cheap, straight-stemmed pipe, reputed by the man who had sold it to him for thirty-five cents to be an Italian briar. He nodded in agreement with Pond's sentiments and lit it.

"I'll wait," he said.

"Thanks," said the cook and housemaid, with heavy irony.

He lifted one of the stovelids, took his wary eyes momentarily off Hayle to peer into his fire, and then picked up a piece of kindling wood and a hatchet. Suddenly he whirled, wrinkled face convulsed, and flung the hatchet with all his might at Roderick Hayle.

"Tryin' again to kill him?" shrieked the cook. "I'll—"

Quick as a leaping cat, Hayle flung himself sideways off the chair. He thumped on the floor. Recovering, he crouched, on hands and bent legs, head toward Pond, who had caught up another missile. He waited, poised, until Pond had hurled a stovelid over his head. Then he darted in. With a short, snapping right to the wry-necked man's chin he knocked all resistance out of him and dropped him onto the box of kindling wood.

The cook's face was still writhing with anger. He glared defiantly up at the tall young man who stood in some perplexity above him.

"Blast you, I ain't afraid of you!" he snarled. "You're the guy that slugged Will an' chucked him into the Sound, ain't you? Well, go on—kill me! I ain't afraid of you!"

"You don't sound afraid of me," Roderick Hayle said soothingly.

He attempted no arguments or denials. Dragging down a length of cord on which a couple of cloths were drying over the stove he started methodically to tie up Pond. The cook's red, blinking eyes clung to Hayle's face save once when, in wonder and some unease, they dwelt upon the silver disk at the back of his head.

"What the hell d'you want with Will Sheppard?" Pond snarled, almost unwillingly. "You can't rob him—he ain't got nothing left!"

"I owe him something," Hayle replied, working steadily

on his job of trussing up his wry-necked captive. "And I'm going to tuck you in a closet somewhere before you start throwing stoves and interrupting us."

Pond received this with wrath. "You figger we'll jump you together—when Will comes," he raged. "I'll bet you're the dirty heel that cracked him on the head at Westport or—"

"The newspapers said it was a wallop from a back-firing prop that got him," Hayle murmured. "Times have changed for Will Sheppard. He used to fly the best ships as fast as they came through the shop. Now what's he flying? Lushing a bit these days, isn't he?"

With head more askew than ever the wry-necked man glared at the man bending over him.

"Tryin' to make me talk, hey?" he snarled. "You'll never get nothing from me but—that!"

His head lunged forward and his teeth closed with a snap only a fraction of an inch from Hayle's swiftly withdrawn hand.

"What would you recommend for a gag?" Hayle asked coolly.

He strolled away from the angry captive to the nearest window and glanced out at the sky, listening. Then, as he started away, he stopped and his eyes fell to the level of the Bay. Although he looked out for only an instant there was a tensity in his gaze that roused Pond's curiosity.

"What you gawkin' at now?" the cook demanded.

"JUST A ROWBOAT," Hayle replied briskly. "You'll be having visitors, Pond, and you're safer tied up. If you're fond of that boss of yours keep quiet about me being around."

He stepped over the prostrate Pond and slipped out onto

the deck without another word. He closed the door with gentle firmness. Swiftly he rounded the corner of the shack and came at once to a ladder nailed to the side of the house.

With instant decision he swung himself up on it. In another moment he was on the roof. He crept over it and lay flat alongside the open skylight, with his head raised. Smoke from the burning bacon on the balky stove below swirled past him, as if out of a chimney.

A single glance over the further edge told him that the rowboat he had seen was now almost against the lower side of the houseboat. There its timbers projected into the shallow water of the rising tide. In the boat were three men. Roderick Hayle stared hard, almost incredulously.

"Where's Fingy?" he murmured uneasily.

In Hayle's underworld life he had known all three of those men in the boat. Even if he had not, he could have appraised them easily enough.

Cannons.

Dropping back beside the skylight Roderick Hayle awaited their approach with a blank face.

At the oars and swinging them clumsily enough, was Hip Bruno, a fat man with an enormous brow and an even more enormous stomach, dressed like something out of a Sixth Avenue show window. In the sternsheets side by side, were Joe Lucci, a smooth-shaven, dark complexioned gentleman in a dark suit that emphasized his glaring yellow shoes, and Moke Wagner, slack-lipped, chinless, stupid.

All of them were moral idiots, no more aware of right and wrong than a dinosaur—and just as witlessly ferocious.

Hayle's face hardened. "Just what I was," he murmured. "Only no operation will change them."

Again his eyes roved about the bay and the shore, looking for some sign of the ever smiling, infinitely more dangerous Fingy Catlin.

The rowboat came alongside with a thump and the three scrambled out hastily. Bruno dropped the painter of the boat over a bit and they rapidly circled the deck. Then to Hayle's ears, came the thud of a foot on wood and the crash of the unresisting door. He raised his head again, this time peering cautiously through the narrow crack between sash and frame of the open skylight.

"Lookut!" It was Hip Bruno's voice. "Somebody's spliced up this guy! Who done it, fella? Are ya alone? Take a look around, you two! How about it, fella? Talk!"

Roderick Hayle slipped his automatic out of his shoulder holster while he awaited Pond's reply. The trio were in sight below him now, standing over the bound captive.

"What're you thugs bustin' in for?" the irate cook snapped. "Think I'm afraid of you, you mangy heels? What's the idear?"

"We got business with your boss," Hip said, and dug his toe into Pond's side with a vehemence that brought a grunt of pain from him. "What we want outta you is answers, not questions. Who done you up?"

Pond's voice rose a trifle louder, as defiant as ever. "A lousy punk—he might ha' been your brother by his looks—stuck me up. He's gone now."

Bruno kicked him again, viciously.

"Take a look, youse!" he blared at his companions. "I told you that twicet! When's your boss due, you?"

"Think I'm afraid of—" Pond stopped with a groan of anguish as Bruno's foot again drove into his ribs.

"Next time I'll put the boots to your nut!" Bruno snarled. "When's your boss due back?"

"Tuesday!" Pond gasped weakly.

"Don't let him fade out on ya, Hip!" Lucci advised, eying the almost fainting cook with a professional eye. "There's nobody else around this joint to give us information."

"Tuesday, hey?" Hip Bruno repeated viciously. He put his foot on Pond's twisted neck and bore down on it. "I just wanted to hear ya lie, Screw-neck! Sheppard left Bridgeport bound this way more'n an hour ago!"

Pond was wailing under the pressure of that inexorable foot yet cursing his torturer in bursts of valiant defiance.

Rod Hayle made no move. He waited, listening tensely.

Hip Bruno lifted his foot. He walked over to a kitchen table under the skylight and scattered a pile of legal looking documents and bound copies of testimony.

"Court junk, hey?" he grinned. "Maybe Sheppard is just studyin' to be a lawyer. An' maybe again he's studyin' to raise hell for somebody. Do like we was told with this stuff, Moke! Don't miss none of it. Y'see, crooked neck—"

"Why tell that baby all the bad news about why we're here?" Joe Lucci broke in.

"Is it goin' ta matter what he knows?" Hip rasped. "You poor zob, d'ya think he's goin' round tellin' people things like what I look like—after we seen his boss?"

The silent Moke Wagner gathered together the papers while Hip Bruno gabbled on. He picked up the piles, walked across the room and hurled them into the stove.

"There they go—up the flue!" said Hip. "All about Fingy an' what a hard guy he is to put a hand on when—"

"You old woman!" Lucci said in disgust. "One o' these

days you'll be chatterin' the same way to the D.A.—only it'll be Moke an' me you'll be talkin' about."

"That's so," growled Moke as he came back from the blazing stove.

"Why, you— Listen!" Hip's voice rose shrilly in sudden excitement—a strange voice from such bulk. "What do ya hear?"

The three men froze, ears cocked, sinister faces intent.

6

NAILED TO A TARGET!

ROD HAYLE, ON the roof, had already been listening to the faint drumming, a sort of accompaniment to Hip's mouthings, for several minutes. He knew it for the slowly rising roar of a plane.

"Slap a plug in this mark's gob an' sling him under a bed, Moke," Hip Bruno commanded. "If that's Sheppard we want ta handle him first. No noise—no gats—just the saps—but hit harder'n Fingy hit him up the Sound. He's got a skull like a rock—but this time I'll crack it for him like an egg!"

A yell from Pond dropped suddenly into a muffled, feeble cry that died away almost at once as Moke bent over him. Next minute Moke dragged him out of Rod's sight, into the bedroom. Pond was gagged as well as bound.

Rod Hayle rolled over onto his back. Among the hurrying cumulus clouds in the northwest a flying boat, cutting altitude rapidly was heading toward the Bay. There were not many of that ancient vintage left in the air; the chances were overwhelming that this was Will Sheppard winging home. And once he stepped into that door—

Hayle's forehead wrinkled. He had never yet heard of one man with a gun getting three.

"If Will Sheppard is even near this houseboat when somebody is killed the cops will hang murder on him sure," he told himself. "Time to—"

But his plans were made for him—below.

"I can't see nothin' through this window," Hip Bruno muttered. "He ought'a be landin'—"

"Try the skylight, then!" Lucci suggested. "Stan'on the— Cripes! Look! That shadow!"

Roderick Hayle had ducked at the man's first words but his shadow on the glass betrayed him. He swung around instantly, on his feet.

A bullet snarled through the glass and left its cold breath on his temple. With a darting glance at the flying boat, already levelling off over the water, he drove his foot through the heavy sheet of glass and sent it crashing down on the table beneath.

A yell from beneath told him that Lucci was in trouble, but again and again bullets sliced past his bent body. His strategic post was gone; he was nailed to a target instead.

On heavy feet he thudded toward the ladder at the edge of the roof. Then, whirling, he crept back, his feet touching like the pads of a leopard. Boldly he sprang clean through the skylight.

The glass littered table beneath held his weight for only an instant. But even as it collapsed he leaped clear. His cold gun warmed to the swift pressure of his finger.

Lucci, pawing at his glass-cut face, was out of it for the moment. Bruno and Wagner were both jumping for the door. They had smoking automatics level in their gripping hands. But the guns were pointed in the wrong direction.

Roderick Hayle got Moke Wagner squarely in the throat

as he turned. Bruno, though he yelped as a bullet creased his paunch, plunged through the door out onto the deck. Despite his bulk he was far the most dangerous with his pistol.

Lucci had given over his ministrations to his face to dive instantly through the window opposite the door. Outside he whipped out his gun and put Roderick Hayle in instant peril of a raking cross fire.

Bruno's gun hand, like the head of a snake, had darted into sight, fired once and vanished again around the edge of the door. Too small a target to waste lead on in that moment when life and death balanced on the scale.

In three bounds Roderick Hayle put the cast iron stove between his body and Lucci's lead. His right leg had a burning hole through it, but it bore his weight as he dropped into a crouch.

Heedless of Lucci's bullets clanging on the stove and of Wagner's death flurry on the floor, Roderick Hayle looked at the door jamb where the automatic had projected momentarily. Hip Bruno had fired and ducked back as Roderick Hayle whirled beside the stove. Now he awaited another chance to fire without peril to himself.

Roderick Hayle grinned mirthlessly, measuring the distance from where the automatic had showed to where Hip Bruno's vulnerable bulk might hide behind the wall.

Hip might be on his knees or standing in the cover of the houseboat's wooden side. He would never risk dropping to his huge stomach in that mix-up.

Methodically Roderick Hayle put four shots into the flimsy wall in the form of a square—two about four feet high, two about three feet high—with the breadth of a man's body between them. It was cool and accurate shooting. Though a couple of shots remained in the gun he slipped out the cartridge clip and shoved in another.

Hip Bruno appeared at the door. He was clutching his chest but it was his legs that appeared to be affected. They twisted and buckled under his weight—the weight they had borne so willingly for many years. And Bruno's face was ludicrous in its dull, perplexed, jaw-dropping amazement at their rebellion.

Suddenly he slid to the floor. He lay there, kicking, entirely conscious.

Out of the bedroom, grotesque in its struggles against the cord that still bound all but one forearm, squirmed the body of Pond. He moved by inches but there was purpose in his dauntless twistings and his half free hand helped him.

Roderick Hayle moved sideways across the room to the door. The stove had ceased to clang; there was no face or pistol in the window where Lucci had been.

But through that window came the thunder of the flying boat as it taxied to the beach beside the houseboat.

THE DECK OUT on which Hayle darted was empty. No swift figure was rushing toward the rowboat.

Then, as he rounded the corner, Lucci was before him. Three-quarters of the way up the ladder to the roof, he was turning head and shoulders as his cocked ears caught Hayle's light footfalls.

Though Lucci fired first, pouring out lead, his cramped arm and twisted body ruined his accuracy. Roderick Hayle's automatic blared only once, but his bullet dropped Lucci from the ladder and laid him, a crumpled, bloody mess, on the deck. He was dead, for Roderick Hayle had aimed, with cold intent to kill, at the head of the venomous thug. Now Hayle stood glancing at the body for a brief tick of time. Destined from birth to be a killer and a curse to his decent fellowmen, Lucci would be an asset to the world in his coffin. Too well Hayle knew that murderous breed. Fate, for a brief time, had made him one of the devil's brew. He knew annihilation was the one remedy.

"Decency that never existed cannot be created by the surgeon's knife," his own savior, Dr. John Arnold, had told him sadly.

The sound of another shot came from within the houseboat.

Swinging on his heel, Roderick Hayle rushed again toward the door. Even as he ran he saw that the flying boat was already running aground on the beach, with motor switched off. The lone occupant, helmeted and goggled, was jumping ashore.

At the door of the houseboat Roderick Hayle stopped. Three figures confronted him in the shambles on the floor. Two did not move. Moke Wagner was dead now. So, too, was Hip Bruno. But the cause of Bruno's death was not the bullet that Hayle had planted in his chest. A hatchet— the weapon Roderick Hayle had dodged—was sunk in his head.

Beside Bruno's huge bulk lay Pond. The wry-necked man was still gagged and bound, save for that one free hand. He was purple in the face, as if from great effort, and his nostrils flared above the taped gag in his mouth. Rod Hayle moved toward him, and jerked clear the gag.

"He tried—kill me—with his gun," Pond panted. "But—I got him—slammed him—with—ax."

"Blast you!" Roderick Hayle said bitterly, walking toward him. "You've stopped the jaw I figured would wag for me—you've plugged a hole I counted on!"

"He ain't—alive and kicking—as they say," Pond retorted tremulously laying his free hand on his wounded side. "That suits me, mister."

Behind Roderick Hayle quick footsteps thudded on the deck. A lean, gaunt-eyed figure in flying kit stood in the doorway, quick glance taking in the scene of slaughter, his bound and helpless servant, and the one man still upright in the room.

Will Sheppard's pause was a matter of a fraction of a second. Then he charged, with empty hands, straight toward Roderick Hayle. Unreasoning fury and reckless courage gleamed in his deep-socketed eyes.

Fast as he was, Roderick Hayle was put to it to dodge those short clutching, vengeful hands as they thrust toward his throat. Side-stepping, he managed to evade the first plunge; then knocked some of the speed out of his new assailant with a swing of his gun.

Will Sheppard staggered. Roderick Hayle gripped his small body before he fell.

"Postpone the berserk fury, Sheppard," the man with the silver plate in his skull said with cold, fire-drenching emphasis. "This is no time for hysterics. Calm down!"

With extraordinary swiftness Will Sheppard came clear of the dual effects of the blow on the head and his own impulsive wrath. The blazing eyes subsided to glowing wrath; he looked with quick perplexity from Roderick Hayle to Pond.

"What's all this, Tim?" he demanded.

"Don't ask me," Pond muttered. "But this tall guy shot 'em all; he dropped this fat slug that kicked my ribs in. But it was me that finished him."

"Thereby cutting a line to the cause of your misfortunes, Will Sheppard," Hayle said in his cool, even tone.

"Misfortunes!" the small pilot cried desperately. "This is worse than that other frame-up! They'll have me in the chair! What—"

"Untie me!" bawled Tim Pond, but neither of the two other living men in the room spared him as much as a gesture.

"Think, man!" Roderick Hayle urged. He walked to the window and flung a hand toward the boats in the bay and the houseboats and shacks along the shore. A few cautious men were already in sight here and there. Doubtless telephones were clamoring for the police.

"Think!" he repeated and hurried on: "The shooting started while you were still in the air; those people know that. No shot was fired after you reached the houseboat. You're clear. But there's no time to talk now; come with me."

Will Sheppard made a gesture of boundless perplexity.

"What's it all about?" he demanded.

"It started in the air—over the Alleghanies," Hayle replied curtly. "For you it's apt to end under the ground unless you move fast. Trust me!"

"I don't doubt—" Sheppard began frostily, but the grip

of Roderick Hayle's hand on his arm halted his voice in his throat.

"Come!" Hayle commanded. "To your ship—before the police come! Your life depends on it, I tell you!"

Will Sheppard planted his feet on the slanting deck of his houseboat with the finality of one making a last stand. His face became a stubborn mask of refusal.

7

A MISSING FINGERNAIL

NOT AN INSTANT longer did Roderick Hayle waste in talk. He hit the aviator a paralyzing, brain wilting blow on the chin with his right fist, bent, flung him over onto his back.

Tim Pond, with a shriek of rage, dragged his bound body toward Roderick Hayle, clawing at him with his free hand. But Hayle's legs swept by untouched. He lunged to the door with Sheppard a limp burden on his shoulders.

On the treacherous footing of the houseboat's warped deck Hayle raced to the lower side; then thudded down into the shallows. His eyes had swivelled alertly this way and that as he emerged. What he saw sent him on toward the flying boat at all the speed he could muster. A policeman had come on the run out from behind a shack on piles near a group of bungalows. Directed by shouts and pointing fingers, he was sprinting through sea grass and sand toward the houseboat.

Sheppard's body pounded on Roderick Hayle's shoulders, as if bent on knocking him flat in the water. But he rushed on, heart flogging in his chest, for he had no fraction of a second to spare.

The cop's whistle shrilled before Hayle was within

twenty feet of the flying boat; even as he flung his burden on board the whistle was reinforced by shots.

With a mighty effort Roderick Hayle braced his shoulder against the flying boat's bow. The heave lifted the hull clear of the sand on which it was grounded. He pushed again, wading into deeper water; then scrambled aboard. The chill northwester, catching under the broad wings of the plane, set it drifting lazily away from the point of land.

With a darting hand Roderick Hayle switched on the ignition; then leaped to the crank of the inertia starter. The motor was still hot. The propeller turned lazily an instant; then jumped as a cylinder fired. It hesitated as the next cylinder missed and, with a heartening roar, disappeared into flickering invisibility.

Roderick Hayle flung himself into the pilot's seat, letting Sheppard's sprawling body lie on the bottom boards as if it had fallen. He right-ruddered sharply; gunned the ship around and taxied at full throttle down wind.

White water gushed over the lower wing; the ship shook ominously under the shocking vibration of the old motor. He pulled his brown felt hat down hard on his head.

Behind, the cop, in the gunmen's boat, was rowing valiantly. But he was far behind now.

Suddenly Will Sheppard stirred; raised a bewildered head. Bending swiftly, Hayle swung his fist again at that vulnerable jaw. Again the aviator collapsed.

Roderick Hayle turned the ship into the wind and opened the throttle. Sluggishly the boat lunged ahead. Then, under the snarling violence of the motor she climbed up onto the step of her hull. She bounced and flogged over the water while the sandspit on which the houseboat rested grew closer with frightful rapidity.

Tense hands on the wheel, Roderick Hayle set himself to rock her off. He got her into the air, felt her drop again; then lifted her off the water once more. She hung there, clumsy as a duck fighting for flying speed.

Suddenly the rowboat loomed ahead. The cop had flung himself flat in the bottom but his red head and spurting gun stuck up belligerently, flouting what looked like instant annihilation.

The heavy hull cleared him by inches; then climbed a few feet higher—enough to pass over the end of the sandy point. Banking gently, Hayle dodged the houseboat. Beyond, he had more water over which to climb. He made altitude and flew west, over the shallows, islands and bridges of the Bay. The wind battered at the top of his hat but he crouched low enough behind the windshield to keep that terrific blast from tearing the hat away and exposing his head to the world.

Steadily westward, still climbing, he held his course. He crossed over Far Rockaway, and over the inlet behind Long Beach.

Will Sheppard revived again. He lifted dull eyes that steadily became more knowing; his lips thinned as he grasped his position and stared at the man at the wheel of his flying boat. Roderick Hayle, blank-faced, nodded; then gave himself entirely to the handling of the ship.

WRATH KINDLED IN Sheppard's eyes; his hands darted in swift impulse to the wheel. He rasped out something that was quite unheard in the rush of wind and the roar of the vibrating motor.

Roderick Hayle ignored him. If his hands tightened a trifle on the wheel or his feet on the rudder bar, no sign of this was given to Sheppard. Plainly enough Hayle conveyed that if Sheppard wanted to grab the wheel and send them hurtling to the sand or water four hundred feet below there was no way by which Hayle could stop him.

Sheppard's hands withdrew from the wheel. His impulsiveness faded before that imperturbable front like ice under hot water. He sat in the seat beside the pilot; his searching, narrowed eyes fixed upon Hayle's face. Minutes passed while Sheppard stared and grimly waited.

Suddenly, over the clearer water beyond the Jones Beach causeway, Roderick Hayle made a gesture indicative of landing. He throttled the motor, banked into the wind and put the boat in a steep glide. Just above the small, hissing wave-tops of South Oyster Bay he leveled off; then gently set the old ship on the water.

With a steady hand he cut the motor and turned his eyes to meet the bitter, hostile gaze of Will Sheppard.

"You wouldn't come so I had to bring you," Roderick Hayle said coolly. "Believe me, it was necessary."

For a long moment the kidnaped pilot continued his scrutiny. The ship drifted slowly in the broad, deserted expanse of the shallow bay. At last Sheppard spoke, grudgingly.

"Necessary to whom? If you aren't crazy, talk!"

"I will," said Roderick Hayle. "You have no reason to trust me, Sheppard. On the other hand, you have nothing left to lose. If I had wanted to kill you your life has been in my hands since I hit you. I have a gun, you know, perhaps you believe I can use it."

"Who are you?"

"Someone who must be left out of the picture."

"Go ahead."

"Somebody tried to kill you up in the Sound off West-port."

"That's so."

"Three thugs came to your houseboat to kill you to-day."

"Perhaps," said Sheppard warily. "Why?"

"Because you've been digging up evidence and hunting for clues about the murder and plane robbery."

"Why should—"

"That robbery, Sheppard, was arranged by a man who wasn't near the spot. He never is near the spot. The only thing he ever approaches is a telephone. His thugs call him the Copper."

Sheppard said nothing to this.

"Somehow there's a hole in that case—a clue that even now might lead to the Copper. Probably that lead would be through the man who did the actual killing and robbery at the emergency landing field—a gentleman named Fingy Catlin."

Into Sheppard's eyes there leaped suddenly a fierce, eager light. "What!" he snapped out. "Fingy, you say—a fellow called Fingy? Why is he called Fingy? Why, man, why?"

Roderick Hayle's brows tightened.

"Catlin is called Fingy, I believe, for the inadequate reason that he has lost the fingernail from his right fore-finger."

"Like that?"

Roderick Hayle looked down at the hand Sheppard extended to him.

The aviator's right forefinger was entirely devoid of a nail.

"Yes," Hayle said slowly. "Very much like that."

8

A LIFE—AND A MOTOR

THE AVIATOR'S BELLIGERENT suspicion went with a rush. Quick thought succeeded it.

"The timing gear of a car chewed that nail off when I was just a kid," he muttered absently. "By God, that's it! I've been wrong! That's it! Clive is no crook."

He swung around and gripped Roderick Hayle's wrist.

"Listen, whoever you are," he said tensely. "Did you follow my trial in the newspapers?"

"I wasn't in this part of the country," Hayle stated quietly. He drew a handkerchief from his pocket and, as Sheppard talked, tied it around the calf of his leg, where a chunk of lead had gone in and out.

"The thing that ruined and almost convicted me was the testimony of a passenger—the one that wasn't murdered, Peter Clive, a carpenter. He swore that after the ship landed I climbed out of the operating compartment, told him I was going to the field keeper's shack to telephone, and disappeared from sight in the whirling snow. I vanished. Understand?"

Hayle nodded silently.

"A minute later a man about my size, with a mask on, came through the snow to the plane, with a couple of others at his back. He had a gun in his hand; he killed the other passenger like you'd kill a fly when he showed fight, and he clubbed Clive himself with the butt of the gun. That man, Clive testified, had no fingernail on his trigger finger. He saw that in the lights of the plane. He swore it on the stand and if there hadn't been one stubborn, unconvinced man on the jury that testimony would have put me in the electric chair."

"The possibility of such a coincidence as two men with mutilated fingers is remote—except in real life," Roderick Hayle agreed.

"But I always thought this Peter Clive was crooked— that he was paid to frame me to save somebody!" Will Sheppard cried. "I'd been put to sleep myself the minute I entered the field house. How could I suspect anything else but a frame-up?"

His face was grim, desperate. "That job—my work in air transport—meant something to me. I wanted to do things in aviation—I had hopes and plans—and they all went west that night. After they'd decided not to try me again I had no job and my lawyers had all my money. I was a pariah. Flying was closed to me—till I scraped up enough to buy this boat. Clive vanished. He was a dead-head passenger that night—an itinerant carpenter who'd worked a few weeks for the company in Frisco. I set to work to clear myself. I dug into every phase of the testimony. I've got a lot of additional evidence, a few discrepancies, but nothing really conclusive. It was mostly on Clive that I hoped to prove my innocence. I was sure he was crooked. But—"

"You located him?"

Will Sheppard nodded. He was despondent, now. "I think so—Clive was born in Bridgeport and he comes back to work every so often. He's due on a job at Rooster Lake, Connecticut, where he lived for a while. He's supposed to turn up there today or tomorrow. But if he's no perjurer— no crook—what's the good of finding him?"

"We've got to find him!" Roderick Hayle declared crisply. "You've done enough digging to get the Copper— and Fingy—on the alert. They've tried twice to kill you, haven't they? That means something."

"It does!" Sheppard cried. "I've got stuff—"

"What you've principally got is the probability that another man with a fingernail gone is the actual murderer. Fingy has a record. Once you tackle the cops with your additional evidence and that fact they'll think of Fingy Catlin. Judging by the Copper's activity in Fingy's behalf, I suspect that Fingy is one crook who knows something about the Copper's identity—the one man in the world who can lead me to the Copper!"

"Then—why not go back—tell the police— Who are you, anyhow?"

RODERICK HAYLE DID not answer that disjointed question. His face had suddenly become as hard and immobile as a sheet of steel. His hand touched the ignition switch, but did not turn it. He looked appraisingly at Will Sheppard; he spoke curtly.

"Why wasn't Fingy Catlin himself running that exterminating party on your houseboat? Why those three brainless cannons—when Fingy should have been there to do a neat job?"

"That's so," muttered Sheppard. "What does it mean?"

"The Copper said he was closing both ends of the case— both ends! That means—"

He jerked his head in a gesture of decision.

"Fingy is up at Rooster Lake today—to kill Peter Clive," he said with conviction. "Maybe we can stop him—if we can get across Long Island and up to Connecticut in a flying boat. Know where Rooster Lake is located?"

"Inland!" said the small pilot. "I know—but it's a small lake and it's a long way inland."

Will Sheppard stared into the questioning, slate-colored eyes of Roderick Hayle.

Both men were pilots. Both knew the peril of attempting to fly over land in a heavy-hulled boat, with half a ton of motor poised on struts above and behind them—ready to come through like a falling meteor at the slightest misjudgment even in a water landing. Both men had heard the erratic throb of that motor—the slap of pistons against scored, carbon-filled cylinders, the skip of a fouled plug, the vibration induced by the worn bearings of the crankshaft. There were a hundred reasons why that motor might fail—only a few why it should carry them through.

"Enough gas?" Roderick Hayle asked crisply.

"Enough," replied Will Sheppard. "Keep the controls."

He leaped to the starting handle as Roderick Hayle turned the switch.

The motor started. This time there was more water ahead for a take-off. Roderick Hayle eased the ship off but it took every rev in the old motor to break her loose from the clutch of the surface.

Once in the air he eased the riotous motor by a notch or two. A life was at stake at the other end but it would not be saved by jerking the motor out of the boat in the first five miles.

With little altitude under him he swept in over Massapequa. For twenty miles the flat surface of Long Island lay ahead.

"If either of us—come through—crack-up—only chance is telephone," Hayle shouted in the aviator's ear. "Maybe get—state troopers—to the lake—find and guard him!"

Will Sheppard nodded, not too hopefully. The lake lay no more than fifty miles ahead—the most likely chance was to fly there. Twenty miles of flat land—eight miles over the Sound—and then the Connecticut hills—with a small lake far inland as their target.

Only five hundred feet of altitude lay under them as the motor thundered on. The propeller churned the air. The boat shuddered like a creature in pain as it thrust its blunt nose through the wind.

OVER A NARROW blue lake cupped in rugged, oak and maple covered slopes, the gray flying boat circled.

More than once on that reckless lunge over the rough countryside the staccato of the motor had been cut by silence sharp as a knife and quite as deadly to the two men crouching in the air-borne hull. But each time a cough and a report had followed that deadly gap in the roar; each time the propeller had swung on; again the motor had hammered out its blaring tune of power.

They had made the lake—but now they circled over it— eying intently the scattered roof-tops of cabins, bungalows and cottages around its edge. The settlement at Rooster

Lake was no city, but it was well spread out. They could afford to waste no time in fruitless inquiries.

Suddenly Roderick Hayle nodded his head, threw the ship around in a steep bank and dived sharply toward the north side of the lake.

"Some excitement down there!" he shouted, and Will Sheppard's own airwise eyes appraised the scene below.

Growing under them as the ship plunged earthward was a house under construction. The raw yellow of new lumber, framed but not sheathed, showed clearly against the brown of earth and green of pines. There were a couple of cars drawn up near the building, which was not strange. But heading toward it on the road around the hillside were a dozen more—and they were traveling fast.

Staring at that half-finished building, Will Sheppard spoke tersely close to Roderick Hayle's ear:

"Peter Clive is a carpenter—up here on a job. Maybe this—best bet"

The man at the wheel nodded agreement; then spiraling once over the shore, set the boat's nose into the wind and landed quickly. Once on the surface he sent the craft taxiing at top speed toward the new building. Both men leaped into the shoal water as the flying boat's hull grounded on the sand.

9

FINGY GETS SET

THEY HAD NEED to ask no questions about what was bringing the rush of cars toward the unfinished house. In front of it, on the grass, lay the stricken body of a man in overalls. His weathered, rough-featured face was turned to the sky, and in its grayness and pain there was the shadow of death.

His chest was a bloody hollow of broken bones. His legs moved spasmodically and he moaned faintly.

Over him bent a calm little man in a black coat. He was adjusting a hypodermic needle. Plainly his only thought was to ease a dying man's pain. And around clustered staring faces.

With scant ceremony the two men from the flying boat broke through the circle.

"It's Peter Clive!" Sheppard groaned. He dropped to his knees beside the carpenter, staring in pity at the crumpled figure.

Fingy Catlin had come and gone.

Roderick Hayle laid a hand on the shoulder of the doctor.

"We must know," he said. "Was this man attacked—or is this an accident?"

"No accident about it!" snapped the doctor. "His boss, who was coming back to the job with some lumber, saw a fellow in a brown suit up on the scaffolding with Peter. This man fired two shots at Peter. He dropped into the cellar onto a pile of rocks."

His quick hand touched the side of the man's throat and they saw a small hole with powder marks around it.

"That's right!" muttered one of the spectators. "I seen the guy shoot!"

"This is my house," added the doctor. "I was close behind the lumber truck—it isn't five minutes since—but nobody could help him."

At that instant Peter Clive, whose dull eyes had focused upon the face of Will Sheppard, spoke feebly.

"Sheppard!" he muttered. "It's Sheppard!"

"Yes—Sheppard," the pilot said. "Easy, now—"

"Sheppard," broke in the dying man. "Sheppard. Listen! I saw his finger—I saw it again—as—he shot. Then I knew—I knew! It—it wasn't you—that time—in the plane."

"No," said Will Sheppard softly. "It wasn't I."

The doctor paused, keen of face, with the hypodermic drawn away from the dying man's body.

"I saw his finger—half the joint gone—besides the—fingernail," the carpenter gasped. "I—I wronged you—testified—and now—done for—he got me—this time."

"Nonsense, Peter!" said the doctor with a brisk impatience that was almost genuine. "We'll have you slapping shingles on this place inside a month."

"And I'll fix the man who shot you," Will Sheppard promised softly. He stood up and broke through the ring with characteristic impulse, drawing with him the carpenter's boss.

The doctor's skillful hands gently thrust the hypodermic needle into the man's exposed shoulder as he spoke those reassuring words. Whether the man's strength went then or the needle's contents acted instantly Peter Clive's efforts to speak ceased and his body relaxed.

"Not a chance!" murmured the physician, shaking his head.

Roderick Hayle's face was bitter as he looked down at this latest consequence of his career of crime. Nevertheless, he suppressed his own emotion and spoke forcefully to the doctor.

"You heard, doctor—you heard what he said—about Sheppard?"

The physician nodded. "I heard—and Peter Clive has told us his story about the trial often enough for me to understand," he said. "You need not fear—whoever you are—that I will not—"

He paused as a motor roared into action. Together they looked beyond the cottage—at the road. A big black sedan was grinding away in low gear—accelerating swiftly. At the wheel was Will Sheppard. He was alone and his deep sunken eyes blazed vengefully in his thin face as he shot away.

"My car!" shrilled an elongated man in golf tweeds.

"I told him we'd telephoned the cops!" the boss carpenter declared. "But he wouldn't wait—he's gone after that killer. He got away in a gray touring car! There's two o' them in it—an' this aviator ain't got no gun!"

A gray touring car! Roderick Hayle had had one encounter with that armored machine.

"How many roads, doctor—how many main roads near here?" demanded Hayle.

The doctor waved a hand to the southward. "Just one—that circles the lake and then runs west to Danbury. That's the direc—"

"Thanks!" said Hayle. For an instant his harassed eyes surveyed the narrow road, and the cars upon it, both halted and in motion. Then he glanced across the lake and without a word rushed toward the old flying boat.

He shoved it off the beach and leaped for the starting crank. The crowd had little time to gape, for the motor caught and Rod Hayle revved it up mercilessly. The blast hit the rudder and the boat reeled around into the wind.

"No gun—and he goes after Fingy Catlin!" he muttered through his teeth as the ship lumbered ahead.

RIGIDLY HE GLUED his eyes to the one break in the wooded hills around the lake. Somebody's narrow lawn—with somebody's house and a flagpole beyond on the rising ground. Only through that gap could he hope to escape out of this pit—only through that gap lay a chance to prevent one more murder from piling up in the terrible chain on the shoulders of Roderick Hayle.

The water of the lake was smooth—it clung to the flying boat's bottom with invisible, clutching hands. With his wheel and throttle he fought that drag of the water and as a catspaw betokening more wind came ruffling toward him he tore the boat loose. It bounced drunkenly, but his arms like tempered steel—yielding yet strong—he held the ship in the air.

The lake shore was coming toward him like the wall of a citadel. Not a foot of altitude did he attempt to gain then. Speed was what he wanted—speed! Inches above the surface, where the air that bore him was thickest; where the whirring propeller would maintain the surest grasp, he kept the ship. Teeth clenched, eyes wary, he watched destruction grow big ahead.

The motor did not miss. The old ship buckled to the job as insensate wood and metal will under the mastery of a man who trusts it. As true as steel is a phrase that describes a motor as well as a sword. Valves, camshafts, connecting rods, pistons and the hard pressed crankshaft did their jobs in a terrific harmony of effort. Full throttle!

The boat reached the edge of the lake. Roderick Hayle slowly drew back the wheel. The nose of the boat lifted.

The craft jammed up the slope toward the house.

Hayle's eyes were on the flagpole. He did not move his rudder to dodge it. Even the slightest pressure of a rudder means a drag—decreased speed.

The right wingtip of the ship cut past the pole. It was a matter of six inches. The ship screamed on, heading dead for the house.

And then Roderick Hayle made his play. He banked the heavy boat to the limit and sent it knifing into the gap between the side of the house and the reaching branches of the trees. One wingtip pointing earthward, one skyward, the ship hurtled through that narrow space.

To Roderick Hayle's overacute senses, the side of the house seemed to drift by as slowly as a cloud. His fingers were as tense on the wheel as snakes coiled to strike; his eyes darted over the slowly revealed space behind the house.

Just a glimpse he had—gardens. His feet thrust at the rudder. The ship reeled around the house. Roderick Hayle was cutting the bank, raising the wing-tip that threatened any instant to hook into the ground. The ship was losing speed.

The motor still hammered on; the craft still answered the controls. He sent it shooting toward the point on the other side of the cleared space behind the house where the trees were lowest. Recklessly he pulled at the wheel; stalled over the barrier with dying momentum, flattened out and fought to hold his scant advantage over the reaching treetops.

In another instant he was clear. He was up out of the bowl in the hills. That fight was won.

It became instantly a mere skirmish. Somewhere ahead, speeding to safety, was Fingy Catlin. And speeding after him—to what?—was Will Sheppard.

Roderick Hayle's eyes focused on the winding ribbon of the road. Though the trees arched over it in many places and it wound cunningly among the shoulders of the hills he had no difficulty in picking out the gleaming white concrete against the green of the country.

Not for a moment did he attempt to follow it. He climbed, until, godlike, he could look down upon the road and dismiss its tortuous curvings; he flew a straight course.

His eyes, however, never left its windings. The boat raced on, minute after minute.

Simultaneously he saw the two cars.

The pace of the first was reckless enough among those

curves and hills. It seemed fast even when viewed from the air, where things appear small and slow. But the second car—the powerful big black sedan which Will Sheppard had commandeered—that car defied death and seemed to flout physical law in its rocket-like progress. Quality that car had, but it had also a crazed man at its wheel.

It was behind—now perhaps half a mile behind—but it was closing up fast.

Roderick Hayle dropped the nose of his boat and shot downward. The focus changed; instead of unreal pygmy cars racing in toyland the drama below became life-size, and involving life. Steadily, despite the cars' speed, his thundering motor and straight course brought him nearer to the race.

In the gray touring car ahead he made out two people—a driver who hung over his wheel, with shoulders swaying and straining at the curves, and a small passenger of lithe movement who was just then climbing from the front seat into the back seat.

He had almost caught up with Fingy Catlin.

Roderick Hayle made out that the big black sedan, rounding a shoulder of a high hill, had come into the vision of the men in the gray touring car lower on the hill.

The flying boat pushed on. Its dive built up its speed; he passed over the roaring black sedan and looked ahead over the side at the gray car.

That was Fingy—the man who had slipped into the back seat. Roderick Hayle, his face grim-set and bitter, recognized the smooth, sure way he moved; the bent shoulders and crouching, cautious body, as he looked backward down the road whirling away under the wheels.

An instant later Hayle made out something else. A glint of reflected fire from something in Fingy's bent arms stabbed at his eyes.

That thing was no automatic—the thing Fingy had braced on the back of the seat. It was a sub-machine gun—a tommy.

Will Sheppard, in that lurching, storming black sedan had as much chance of drawing even with that gray car, to ram or sideswipe it, as a puppy might have against a panther. A man may not go untouched through a shower—whether it is a shower of rain or a shower of lead.

But he would try it. Hayle, knowing the impulsive, never-surrender character of that pursuing avenger, knew that.

10

THE DECISION OF SILVER SKULL

RODERICK HAYLE HAD a decision to make in that instant. Below was Fingy Catlin, the sly, ruthless, the man of insatiable blood lust who killed as if for pleasure.

Caught, Fingy would talk. With the chair looming he would gush words like a fountain. And Hayle suspected with good reason that Fingy was the Copper's point of contact with the minions of crime—the one vulnerable spot in the Copper's armor of anonymity.

But before Fingy could be caught he would fight like a cornered rat. Before Rod Hayle could expect to lay a hand on Fingy, Will Sheppard's life would go down the wind. The pilot in that whirring, lurching black sedan behind the touring car would die if Fingy lived another sixty seconds.

A lead to the Copper was Roderick Hayle's one aim in life. Such a clue might well mean the elimination of a great power for evil in the world.

But Will Sheppard was a valuable man. He had gone through hell without being beaten. Better planes would fly on safer air lines if Will Sheppard lived and came back, as was his right. A great power for good was that wild, impulsive, brainy flyer.

"It isn't sure that I could take Fingy alive!" muttered

Roderick Hayle. "Even if I did the Copper might get me first—as Dr. Arnold warned me."

Masterfully Roderick Hayle made his decision and ironed out the bitter disappointment on his face. He looked down with hard, implacable eyes. This was the end of his road. A quicker end than he had expected, but in justice he should have finished months before in the electric chair. He did not count in this decision.

"You've got to die, Fingy!" he said.

Before the words were out of his mouth he was diving full throttle at the touring car.

Though the man with the submachine gun, busy preparing to annihilate his victim, had been aware of a plane somewhere high overhead he had given it no attention. Planes did not concern him. But suddenly, as the flying boat, with motor revving its thundering might, shot down, he realized that he had against him not only a mere target on the road but also an enemy in the sky.

With smooth precision he jerked up the deadly tommy.

A flying object is hard to hit—unless it is moving in a straight line toward the man with the weapon. That is what the flying boat was doing.

Roderick Hayle knew what was coming. But with feet braced on the rudder and hands tight on the wheel his body was set to take a few leaden jolts from that submachine gun without losing control.

Fingy Catlin cut loose. Bullets tore through the hull. They snarled past Roderick Hayle's head, rigidly twisted over the side to gauge his plunge. They spattered on the motor and ripped through the wings. Unhurt, Hayle drove on down to the crash.

The driver of the car, jerking his head around, saw the diving plane high astern. It was hurtling at him like a meteorite. Though a curve loomed and the grade was a sharp descent his foot stamped convulsively on the throttle.

The car surged down the hill. It never reached the curve.

Roderick Hayle, flying untouched through space, raised the bow a bit as the car slipped out from under the diving ship. He was flying almost level as he jammed the heavy hull of the boat down on the car. It struck hard, as a dropping flatiron might come down on a walnut.

Tires blew and axles snapped under the impact. The body of the car flattened out on the road—telescoped into its own chassis.

Nor did the flying boat escape destruction. Struts buckled and part of the old hull disintegrated in a flurry of shattered wood as the gas tanks jammed through the bottom. The motor, torn from its bed between the wings, by the shock, hurtled forward, almost grazing Rod Hayle's body, tightly braced against the side of the hull.

Like a meteor the huge mass of metal smashed into the concrete of the road. Its momentum almost completely buried its bulk just in front of the wreckage of the car. The wings sagged and crumpled on either side of the car.

Dazedly Roderick Hayle realized that he was still alive. That last minute spurt of the car's driver had saved him. He had been forced to change his headlong dive into the car to a flatter descent. He had pancaked on it instead of hitting bow on.

Nevertheless Fingy Catlin was dead. Dragging his numb body out of the crumpled chaos Roderick Hayle saw that. Something, probably the gas tank, had come down like the knife of a guillotine as Fingy's upturned head projected over the steel armored rear panel of the car. He was almost decapitated. The hot machine gun lay somewhere beneath his crushed body.

Beside the car lay the driver. His skull had cracked on the concrete and his legs were pinned in the car.

Painfully Roderick Hayle crept down onto the road and, on hands and knees, clutched at a wing strut. His head was reeling giddily. He was not hurt. He knew that. But his weary body was rebelling forcefully against further effort—it fought, after all he had gone through, against doing anything.

With the last of his will power Hayle came to grips with his laggard, fainting body in the hardest struggle of all.

The motor was blazing fiercely in its self-dug pit but no sign of fire showed in the inextricable, gasoline-soaked wreckage of car and flying boat.

THE BLACK SEDAN hummed down the hill and stopped, brakes moaning, in a dry skid that carried it almost into the wing against which Roderick Hayle was leaning. Slowly he got up and faced the deep, peering eyes of Will Sheppard.

"There's your evidence, Sheppard," he said with an effort. His throat was dry as old leather. "You'd better—get Catlin out—before that finger burns up."

But Will Sheppard stopped, staring awe-struck at the man with the silver disk in his skull. "Hurt badly?" he whispered as Roderick Hayle climbed to his feet. "That was a landing, that was."

"A good landing," Rod Hayle said curtly, through tight lips. "Any landing's good you can—walk away from."

He did walk toward the black sedan.

Will Sheppard turned and walked beside him, with a solicitous arm around his waist.

"Help me up," rasped Roderick Hayle. "Into the driver's seat—the driver's seat, I said!"

Almost mechanically Will Sheppard obeyed that commanding, almost arrogant voice.

"Stay here till the cops come," Hayle said to the aviator.

"You'd better let me drive you to the hospital," Sheppard said.

"I don't go to hospitals," Hayle croaked.

"But—look here— What's the idea of— I've got to thank you for—"

"Thanks? No!" said Roderick Hayle. His voice was recovering something of its calm strength. His hand thrust the gear lever into second speed.

"No thanks from you, Will Sheppard. Forgiveness! I was the pilot in the G.M.'s stolen plane that night over the mountains—the fellow that waved you down to that death trap on the emergency field—and was set to force you down if you didn't obey. Forgiveness!"

Roderick Hayle let in his clutch and the black sedan leaped forward, down the hill.

Roderick Hayle had still a goal to achieve—alone.

Before that car was found, in a pasture near a railroad line ten miles away, Roderick Hayle, by box car, trolley and bus, had made his way back to New York City. He crept like a weary, wounded animal into the latest of his temporary shelters—a two room flat in a cheap apartment building.

Recuperating alone, he read with satisfaction the blazing, first page headlines of a nine day sensation wherein

Will Sheppard established his innocence and won back his standing in the Airspeed Corporation.

But Roderick Hayle read, also, that Lump Engel had been released on $5,000 bail—cash bail—pending his trial on a charge of violation of the Sullivan law.

The bitter with the sweet! Roderick Hayle had no fear that the Copper would raise a hand against Will Sheppard now, for any chance of tracing his connection with the case had died with Fingy Catlin. The Copper was too insensate and emotionless a creature, or was he too cautious?—to desire dangerous vengeance.

But—cash bail for Lump Engel! There seemed no chance of tracing the source of that cash—or the source of the cash that would pay Lump Engel's lawyer.

Nor was there ever a chance that Lump Engel, even on the grill of an official or a private third degree, could point the way to the menace who hid behind a telephone.

Doubtless, Lump, when free, would get orders again—but he would never know whence they came. A man as stupid, as crooked, as obedient and incurious as Lump Engel was a useful tool.

Lump would get orders...

Roderick Hayle sat up a trifle straighter in his rickety old armchair and with a thin hand took out of his pocket a sheet of paper with a list of names on it. He crossed off one and looked without despair and without hope at the others.

"Getting the Copper is a luxury—and the decent drudgery of reparation must be done before I can afford luxuries," he warned himself. "But of course if the two jobs should happen some time to coincide—"

www.ingramcontent.com/pod-product-compliance
Lightning Source LLC
Chambersburg PA
CBHW072355030726
47505CB00014B/1846